THE KINGS OF CANTIUM

Book One

ERICA OLSON

The Kings of Cantium is a work of fiction. Names, characters, places, and incidents are the products of the author's imagination or are used fictitiously. Any resemblance to actual events, locales, or persons, living or dead, is entirely coincidental.

Text © 2013 Erica Olson

Cover photo © 2011 Dmitriy Cherevko
Dreamstime.com

Approximately 27,000 words

www.erica-olson.com

First published by Erica Olson, 2013

ISBN-10: 1475106602
ISBN-13: 978-1475106602

Printed in the United States of America
by CreateSpace

For my family

CONTENTS

PROLOGUE

*T*hese are the chronicles of Imon Uliac. I have come here in the night, to the hill of my ancestors; I hope no one has seen me. If they find these pages, they will burn them. But I must press on.

We have forgotten our stories: how it was before roads, before cities, before all this land was tamed. That was before the enemies came and changed us. Now we are like them.

But I remember. My father told me, and my grandfather told him. I am her heir.

For the sake of humanity, she stood against them; others followed. Long dead now, of course. But here I walk where they once walked, hunched against the cold, wet wind. I can almost imagine that I'm one of them, though the defeat they feared came long ago.

The town below is distant; in the darkness, it does not exist. What shall I write of now, beneath the stars? I'll write

of war, of hope, of the ancestors.
    With my words, I will redeem us.

ONE

sa's cousin, Denn, was the first to see them. He'd been off beyond the fields where the river crossed a willow grove, gathering reeds for the bundles of hay. Probably, too, he'd sat on a rock, dipping his toes in the glittering water. Here was no one to tell him he must work faster, must help with the harvest all day in the sun. He was five years old, and the river soothed him.

But what was that? A grunt, some human voice close at hand. Denn crept forward through the willows, the tinkling water muffling his steps. At an opening in the branches, he saw a man dressed in red, with a metal hat and a metal breast. Denn crouched down low. More men were near the first, and Denn could see some sort of camp behind them. At least, he thought it was a camp; the huts didn't look like any in the land of June. Their roofs were flat, their sides were square. Denn couldn't tell for sure, but it seemed like they were made of wood.

The men in red were big and scary. Denn inched back through the willows, then ran as fast as his little legs could carry him.

Isa was in the fields. The sun burned hot on her bare arms, baking her sweat into her skin. Her back ached, but the sun would shine for many more hours, and still she'd be slicing her iron blade through the hay.

Isa wasn't supposed to swing the scythe, of course. She should have walked behind and filled her skirt, piling the cut hay into little mounds, leaving the swinging to the men. But Isa was strong. Why, her brother Tuni said when people complained, should such strength be wasted? Work hard, work hard. Today, as every day, Isa longed for the night, when the moon shone high in the summer sky and the people danced by their fires.

"Isa! Isa!" cried little Denn, gasping as he ran up beside her.

"What is it?" she asked. But for a long moment, he was unable to answer, too winded by his sprint from the river.

"Strangers," he finally got out. "Lots and lots of them. With weapons."

Isa hovered over him. "Where?"

"Down by the bend in the river."

Strangers, on occasion, would come to the land of June, trading their baskets or bowls or gems for sweet summer hay. Isa tried to tell him this, but Denn was adamant. No ordinary strangers, these. They were tall and had odd houses. Thousands of them, Denn thought. And hard to kill in all that metal.

Isa sighed and laid down her scythe. These didn't sound like the river people, nor the scrapers from the salt plain. Likely Denn was mistaken. Still, she'd better tell her brother, Tuni, or he'd scold her later. She patted Denn's head and sent him off home, toward the southern fields. Aunt and Uncle would be reaping still, too harried to stop for a little boy's chatter. Never mind; he could sit by the hut, take a nap, maybe have a barley soup ready for them when they finished. Isa herself headed west, toward the sunset shrine and her brother.

This time of year, the fields were plump and golden, and everywhere sun-bronzed men toiled with their scythes. Women in lightweight sleeveless dresses stuffed their skirts with the cuttings. Everyone knew Isa, and she knew them; she nodded in greeting as she passed. Each of them, whether man or woman, had hair like hers: long, light, and tangled. They were short, though, while Isa was almost as tall as her brother, Tuni, who she found scything in a small hollow.

"Denn saw strangers," she told him, stopping just out of reach of his blade. "He thinks there's danger."

Zing! Zing! sang the scythe. "What strangers?" Tuni asked, hardly stopping.

Isa explained about the big men with the metal helmets and square houses.

Zing! Zing! went the scythe. "Doubt there's reason to worry," said Tuni.

But by dusk, even he was anxious, as more reports came in about the strangers. Old Nel, who lived near the river, had seen them when she'd gone to wash her rags. Someone else had found some willows chopped down, with nothing left but stumps. One man had even spoken to the strangers – or rather, had given a yip of surprise when he emerged, dripping wet and stark naked, after bathing in the river and by accident came out upon their camp. The strangers offered no word of who they were, and the man of June didn't wait to ask them.

An open council was called – a rarity. Though everyone was spread out and busy with the harvest, a great many people came. Isa and Tuni, walking straight from the fields to the sunset shrine, had to elbow their way through the crowd to get a good place. Even Isa's father and mother were there, having walked from the smithy far across the eastern fields.

Confusion ruled for a few minutes as people buzzed

about the strangers and looked around for the members of the regular council. Finally, the old men assembled and Isa's father was called to perform the ritual of blessing. Limping forward, he lit the kindling in the bowl of the sunset shine, the fire burned, and the meeting was under way.

People argued about what to do. Some wanted to tell the strangers to leave, while others demanded more information about them. "We don't have information," Tuni said. "We know nothing about them."

"Send scouts?" someone suggested.

But the issue was soon settled, as the strangers themselves came to the council.

There were three of them, each in a red tunic under a shining breastplate. Their helmets curved down from the forehead to cover the nose, leaving their eyes shadowy and indistinct. The helmets made the strangers appear taller than they were: really they were just a few inches taller than the average man of June, and a head taller than the women, excepting Isa.

At first the people of June were silent; then many babbled at once. Where had they come from? Who were they? Had they come to trade?

One of the strangers, a middle-aged man with a bristly chin, raised his hand for silence. Then he began to speak. Isa moved forward, straining to hear, but even when she was close up she didn't understand. The words were in a strange, garbled tongue that sounded like water running over a bed of pebbles. In all her life, Isa had heard only the language of June and the guttural pidgin from the salt plains.

The stranger stopped speaking and glanced behind him. Then Isa noticed the little stooped form in a woven reed tunic: one of the river people who spent their days hauling in fish and braiding grass nets, not far from June.

The river man cleared his throat. "He says," he squeaked out, "that this land is now the property of the Remi. You will live as before, but will cede what space is needed for the Remi towns, and hand over one-third of your crops."

Some in the crowd erupted with outrage; others laughed. What madness was this? Men shouted challenges at the river man, who held out his hands and said something that Isa couldn't catch. Isa's father waved his arms for silence. People pressed forward, trying to hear the words of the elders and the bleating of the river man.

Isa shifted restlessly. Her legs were sore from the day's work. She wanted to sit, or sleep, or dance by the fires; anything but gawk at these silly men with their helmets and metal shirts. Harmless fools. And look at the people of June: the sweaty farmers; the women in their dirty dresses; Isa's father the smith, leaning on his good leg. All in an uproar. Why did they argue with these strange men? June never changed. Generation upon generation, grandfathers and mothers and sons, had worked in these ripe, rolling fields.

"How about this, Isa?" whispered Nuler, the potter, in her ear. "We're in for trouble."

Isa smiled faintly. Poor Nuler. Isa's mother was always pressing her to marry him. But he was weak, and complained about the heat, and had to take breaks when he was scything. "They don't look so scary to me," she said.

"Right. No," Nuler said hurriedly.

Isa threw back her head. The first stars were peeping out; she could have traced them with her finger. Normally she loved nights like this, when the heat sank to the ground and the people stopped work at last. Then they'd gather around the fires, letting the night cool their steaming skin, and sing the old songs of June. The young ones, like Isa, would whirl in a mad dance, their only reward for long hours of toil in the hot sun.

The crowd had quieted somewhat, and Tuni stepped forward. Isa straightened with pride and scanned around. Yes, all the women were looking at him: tall, solemn, noble Tuni, Isa's golden brother. The old men respected him, though he was not yet thirty, and let him sit on their councils about harvest, winter, and seeding. The unmarried women, Isa noticed, smoothed their hair on the chance that he'd glance their way. Metal strangers be damned; each woman fawned before Tuni, hoping he'd choose her as his wife. But he had chosen none of them as yet, so Isa kept his fire.

Now Tuni spoke gently, patiently. "What right have the Remi to come into June?" he said. "Who are the Remi to demand land and tribute? During harvest, no less, when all are busy and tired. Leave in peace, and June will let you alone." The people around murmured in agreement; Isa gazed adoringly at her brother. "If the Remi need food," Tuni added, "we have food in abundance. We would be happy to trade with the Remi, if the Remi have something to trade. But you must wait until after the harvest. We work from dawn to dusk, and have no time for trade."

Isa watched the stooped little river man tilt his head toward the strangers, listening to their burbling words. The river man nodded rapidly, but he made no reply to Tuni. Astoundingly, one of the Remi men spoke instead. "No trade," he said roughly. "Take. We take from you."

The people of June whispered amongst themselves. Isa frowned. She could understand the river man having learned the tongue of his conquerors. But this Remi stranger – surely he hadn't heard the language of June before.

"No trade," the Remi man said again. "We take."

"That's ridiculous," cried Batt, barging past the elders to place himself in front of the Remi. "The three of you, against all of us? A squirrel beats a bear, more likely."

Batt was Isa's other brother. Four years younger than Tuni, he was yet five years older than Isa, who was nineteen. He had a wife, Maive, and several small children. Isa scowled at him now. She wanted to tell him that these three were just a sampling; the Remi had a whole camp by the river. But as usual, Batt failed to see the obvious.

"You Remi are women," he said loudly. "I'll cut you down myself."

Quicker than Isa could draw a breath, the lead Remi's sword flashed and Batt was on the ground. He yelped and held his head; a thin trail of blood ran from his cheek. Several men of June rushed forward to his defense, but of course they had no weapons, having come straight from the fields. The three Remi easily deflected them, grouping together in a triangle with their swords pointed outward. In time, perhaps, the crowd could have overcome them, but the Remi left no chance of that: as abruptly as they came, they melted into the night.

"We will send to our allies," Tuni shouted. Isa jumped; Tuni was never loud. "The river people, the salt traders. They will come."

The river man, who still stood in the council circle, shook his head. "The river people are conquered," he said sadly. "As for the people of the salt plains: they were the first to meet the Remi, after they crossed the wide waters in their wooden ships. First to meet them, and first to die." He shook his head again, crinkling his eyes at Tuni. "You must give in. It's the only way."

TWO

*I*n the first days, the Remi kept to themselves in their camp by the river. Bridge Town, they called it. The occasional Junian would sneak down through the willows and see the square houses, the iron forges, the felled logs laid across the river. Maybe, some said, the Remi would live there and leave the rest of June alone. Small price to pay, for letting them have the river land. But soon the Remi began to expand their domain. They traveled far into the fields, marking certain hills for their possession. Between these hills and their river camp, they dug wide trenches across the fields, which they used as thoroughfares for quick travel.

The people of June had never had roads. They stored their food in the fields where it grew, and had few other moveable goods. Now, though, the Remi had something to transport: the stone they quarried from their hills. With it they made buildings to replace their original wooden ones.

In June, stone houses were an impossible luxury. With all the labor spent on wheat, hay, and barley, the people had no time for quarrying. But the Remi didn't have to worry about feeding themselves. They built in stone in Bridge Town, which was rapidly expanding, and also at crossroads in the fields. At these stations, the Remi collected food from the surrounding June farmers: one-third of the crop, as the river man had said at the council.

Many small skirmishes erupted when the Remi began to take land and food – but only with those who happened to be in the particular field at the time. The Junians made no concerted attack, all gathered together, until the week after the harvest was complete.

That morning, Isa was walking with her brother, Tuni, to fetch bowls for grinding grain from Aunt and Uncle. As they passed the sunset shrine, they noticed a small party of Remi gathered with buckets and iron hoes.

"What are you doing?" asked Tuni. "That's a shrine."

"None of your concern," said one of the Remi. "Move along."

All of the Remi could now speak fluently without a translator, though it was scant weeks since they'd first heard the language of June. Isa couldn't understand it. One day she'd asked the little river man, who remained in June, how long it had taken him to learn the strange Remi tongue.

"Oh, months and months," said the river man. "And you know what's odd? They picked up our river speech right away."

Isa bit her lip. "How could they learn it so fast?"

The river man shrugged. "They're smart."

Isa shook her head. "But it's not just the language. It's everything. Their houses and clothes and swords. Have you seen the metal they use in their swords?

"Yes," said the river man. "They call it steel."

Isa knew this. "But how did they figure out how to

make it?"

The river man glanced around before replying. "They have a secret weapon," he said in a low voice. "I haven't seen it, but some of my people talk of it."

Isa raised an eyebrow. "What weapon?"

"Some kind of plant that they found," whispered the river man. "They eat it, and it makes them like gods."

Isa frowned. "What do you mean?"

The river man shook his head. "I don't know exactly. But it makes them smart. Unnaturally smart. Beyond human."

Strange little man, Isa thought as she walked away. Could his explanation be true? Already, the Remi had solved problems it took Junians years to work through, like diverting water from the river. For generations, June had relied upon the natural cycle of storms to replenish the crops. Then, when Isa's father was a boy, a few men dug a trench to funnel water from the river to the eastern fields. The trench made the fields more resistant to drought, but it was unpredictable at best. Then the Remi built a massive stone dike. Most days, it held back the waters of the river, but when the Remi so willed, they opened a hatch and immersed the fields. Witchcraft, said Nuler, the potter. Isa doubted the Remi were witches, but they knew many things the Junians did not.

Now, the Remi party told Tuni and Isa to move along as they dug up the sunset shrine, making room for some new road or building. Isa feared that Tuni would do something rash and get himself hurt, but he only stood there mutely, lips pursed, as the Remi knocked over the ritual bowl and chipped away the standing stone. Then Tuni took Isa's arm and led her away.

Ages upon ages, Junians had worshiped at the sunset shrine, rejoicing in the bright days that brought the wheat and hay and barley. By late morning, dozens of men had gathered at Tuni and Isa's roundhouse, conferring angrily.

"They told me they wanted it for collecting grain," said Batt. He had an ugly red scar on his cheek where the Remi sword had struck that first night. "I said, that's not farmland. You don't need it."

Isa leaned against the outside of the house. The straw was warm on her back. *Sweet land of June!* she thought. Grass and blossoms still stuffed the fields; birds still sang in the hay. But June was changing, and Isa dreaded what it would be.

The men of June attacked in mid-afternoon, when the Remi laid down their building tools and rested near their houses, feet stretched out in the shade. Isa's father had forged new weapons, anticipating this conflict with the Remi. But he'd had little time. The harvest had kept him busy with his usual work of repairing scythes for the fields. When he did make a sword, he could hardly get the fire hot enough to mold the iron; the Remi had cut down most of the trees he used to stoke the flames. So the Junians had meager weapons when they marched to battle.

Of the three hundred who went to Bridge Town to fight the Remi, only a few dozen limped back across the fields. The least hurt carried those worse off. Three of them brought Tuni to Isa, unconscious, his stomach gaping open. Then Isa wished for the lost days of summer, when the Remi only made cuts in the fields.

For a few days, Tuni tossed and turned with fever, which gradually abated. But still he didn't recover. No longer in immediate danger of death, he lost his fervor for life. Isa sat and sang to him, and fed him bread, and held up his cup when he wanted a drink. Mostly he stared straight ahead, not seeing her, mumbling his thanks when she adjusted his blanket. Occasionally he would talk, if visitors came, but the effort left him so exhausted that these guests never stayed long.

If only Isa could have born to change his bandages. She tried, desperately wanting to help him, but the moment she lifted the cloth and saw the tangled pit of gooey flesh, she had to run outside and vomit in the grass while their brother, Batt, finished the dressing. Batt came often. He would fuss about the smoke from the fire, which Isa lit indoors to keep Tuni warm. Then he'd hurry away, afraid to leave his wife and children alone for long; with good reason.

After the battle, the Remi had cracked down on June. Now the stations at the crossroads were not just for grain, but for weapons. Soldiers piled in, trying to cow the people and impress them with Remi strength. Whenever Isa walked to the well beyond the ruined sunset shrine, soldiers were standing there, sullen, their unnatural swords glimmering in the sun.

"Someone must go for help," she said one day in the roundhouse.

"Where?" asked Batt irritably. "The river people are wiped out. The Remi are everywhere. Everyone's the same as us."

Isa pulled at her hair. "Are there no people beyond the river?"

"Yes," said Tuni from his bed of reeds. "But they're scattered. Each little group has its own field to live on. People don't cluster together anymore."

"We do," said Isa.

Tuni coughed. "We of June are the only ones. Even we're spread far and wide. It takes miles of walking to gather us all. Not like years ago, when this land was crowded with too many people, as we hear tales of. Then every settlement butted up against another, and people went hungry. They fought wars to get food. But not us. There aren't so many people now. Until now, there's been little danger."

"What happened to all the people?" Isa asked. "Why are there so few of us now?"

Tuni shrugged. "Disease?" he suggested.

Batt spat into the fire. "Maybe they all killed each other. Gods hope so, anyway. More room for us."

Isa thought for a moment. "What about Cantium?" She had heard of the kingdom of Cantium as a child. Long ago, it had been a great center of culture, spreading its influence throughout the land, even down to June, which was just a client kingdom then. But Cantium had produced more than songs and stories; its greatest strength was in war.

Batt laughed roughly. "Yes, there's an idea, Isa. An old hill town that's been dead for hundreds and hundreds of years."

Isa glared at him. "How do you know it's dead?"

"Think about it," said Batt. "They were our allies. People from Cantium came to June, and we went up there to trade with them. Then they stopped coming. Why do you think we don't trade with Cantium anymore? It doesn't exist."

But Isa persisted. "How could a great kingdom just vanish? Maybe there's something left, anyway. Fragments of what it once was."

"Unlikely," said Batt.

"Still, it's possible," Isa said. "Someone should go and find out if it's still there. That's our only chance."

Batt smirked at her and said nothing.

"Ask them, Isa," Tuni said weakly. "Ask around, all the men." He broke into a fit of coughing; Isa watched him worriedly and held his hand. "But I fear," Tuni said when he could talk again, "that you'll find no one to go. We of June aren't wanderers. We're a home people. When was the last time someone walked more than a few days away from here? I can't remember; not in my lifetime."

Isa asked everyone. But as Tuni predicted, she could find no man for the task. They just stood and stared at her like she had sprouted an extra head. "Cantium!" cried Nuler, who Mother wanted her to marry. "That must be years away. And giants live there. My grandmama told me."

"I've got the family to think of," said Uncle, his arm around little Denn, who had scratched himself badly in some briars. "I can't go."

Oh, but someone must! Isa thought as she stumbled home across the fields. She could feel June slipping away. The songs beneath the stars – now they never sang them. Of all the options she could think of, only one seemed possible. She would go to Cantium herself.

"I forbid you to go," Batt declared. "It's not safe."

"It's not safe here anymore," Tuni pointed out.

"Then marry her off to someone," Batt snapped. "A husband would protect her."

Wearily, Tuni shook his head. "Our way of life is ending. Someone must go."

"It's no business for a woman," Batt growled.

But Isa lived in Tuni's house, so Tuni won. She would go in search of Cantium. Tuni would stay at the smithy, where Mother and Father would care for him while Isa was gone. That very next day, Aunt and Uncle came to help Batt and Isa carry him. All of them were strong, especially Isa, but it was a long slog across the fields with Tuni on a blanket between them. As much as they tried to be gentle, inevitably they jostled him as they walked. He clenched his teeth and bore it. When they finally arrived at the smithy, his face was white and his eyes were closed. Gingerly, they transferred him onto Mother and Father's bed.

Isa knelt beside him. Brushing back her long hair, she bent over and kissed his forehead. "I have to go now," she whispered.

Tuni opened his eyes and smiled weakly. "Yes. Do well, little sister."

Isa ran out of the hut so that he wouldn't see her cry.

Dear June! she thought as she walked north through the fields. *What will you be when I come back?* A worry that should not have bothered her in these sweet last days of summer; but everything had changed. She looked at the land and hugged it to herself, trying to take it with her in her mind.

Then her face darkened. Even these far fields bore scars

from the Remi: crumbled rocks, fresh-dug ditches, piles of hewn-out soil. A secret weapon, the river man had said; some kind of plant that they had discovered. She, Isa, would find out what it was that gave them unnatural intelligence. She would find out, and she would stop them.

THREE

The fields of June gave way to vacant hills, where thistles pricked through Isa's shoes. She walked briskly, the bottom of her dress whisking through the grass: Swish swish! Swish swish! The silence disconcerted her; she was used to people, activity, voices. To pass the time, she sang old haying songs:

> For how many years
> Has the grass rested in the sun?
> For how many years
> Has light streaked this hallowed ground?
> Sun-baked hands swing
> Swift blades in the striped summer fields,
> Bringing sweet smells of fresh cut hay.
> For how many years?
> For how many years?

It was almost noon when she saw a single roundhouse,

almost hidden in a bank of briars. A man and woman emerged, beckoning to her and smiling broadly.

"Hello!" called the man. "What brings you here? We don't often get visitors this way."

"I've come from June," said Isa. "We've been invaded, and I'm looking for help. Do you know the way to Cantium?"

"Cantium?" said the woman. "Oh, my. No one's lived there for a thousand years."

"Sooner than that," Isa said patiently. "They were allied with June."

"In any case, it's dead now," said the man. "I have no idea how you'd get there."

"All right." Isa sighed. "Thank you, though."

"Are you hungry?" the woman asked.

Isa glanced at the sun. "A little, but I really must be going. I want to walk a good deal today."

"Wait," the woman said. "You're not leaving until you've had a good meal." She disappeared into the house.

Isa started to inch away. "I have such a long way to go."

The man clapped her on the back. "Come! Share in our hospitality. What kind of people would we be if you didn't?"

Isa sighed and waited for the woman. No use hurting their feelings. She quickly gulped down the food when it came.

It was evening before she saw people again. A few roundhouses perched atop a knoll, which was so covered in stones that Isa tripped twice as she climbed it. A woman came out of a house and stared at her.

"Hello," said Isa. "I'm looking for the kingdom of Cantium. Do you know the way?"

The woman looked her up and down, but didn't answer. Three more people came out of the houses: two girls and a boy. They too stared at Isa. She looked back at them, thinking they'd be abashed when caught staring, but they kept on with no shame. Hadn't they seen a stranger before? It was like they'd never lived in a community of people. Isa asked again for Cantium.

"We don't know," said the woman. "Go away."

How strange, thought Isa as she continued along through the hills. *The Cantians once ruled this land, all the way down to June, and now there's not a trace of them.*

The days rolled on like that. At night, she curled up to sleep in a hollow or beneath a bush before pressing on once again. Rarely did she see people more than one or two times a day. She'd go to them, begging for food, and they'd give her some bread or meat, or a few apples from a wild tree. Then she'd ask about Cantium. At first they shrugged and shook their heads, but gradually she came upon people who knew – or claimed to know – something of it. No, they hadn't been to Cantium themselves, but they'd met someone who had. "My friend's cousin was there once," they'd say. "No, there's nothing left. Nothing but grass and the wind." But what was the truth, really? Isa had to hope.

As the days passed, June seemed ever distant. Gone were the golden fields and sun-tanned threshers; here the weather was rainy. Once, a storm caught her atop a high ridge. She watched the clouds roll in across the plain, black with foreboding, lightning flashing in their crowns. There was no time to descend the hill, so she ran madly, exposed to the wind, finding shelter in an ancient ditch near the hilltop. There she crouched, cold and wet, while the storm raged around her and thunder rang in her ears.

One day she came to a break in the uplands where the ground sank to a sandy bog. The air was noxious, like something large had died there. But four roundhouses stuck out of the mire, sagging pitifully, their sides bleached pale like the sticky soil all around. No one came out when Isa called. She didn't want to wade through the muck to check if anyone was inside, so she turned to leave. Probably no one had lived here for years.

"And who are you?"

Isa almost jumped out of her shoes. The man was standing quite near her, blending in so well with the marsh that she hadn't seen him. His clothes were tan and sandy, as was his hair. Even his face was smeared with the dry, light mud, making it impossible to tell how old he was: he could have been sixteen, or sixty, under that grime. He stepped closer. Isa's nose wrinkled; he stank of marsh grass and putrid water.

"Who are you?" he repeated.

Isa stared back coldly to cover her embarrassment of being startled. "I am Isa Uliac of the land of June."

The man stared at her. He had big, bulging eyes with heavy lids. Isa thought of frogs. "June?" he said. "Sounds odd. Never heard of it."

Isa picked up her heels, which where sinking in the bog. "We're a great farming people."

Frog Man blinked at her, a smile playing on his lips. "Not as great as here, I suspect. We pull five shocks of rye a summer out of here. They have me, of course. Without me they wouldn't get half as much. The other day, I cut a water root the size of my wrist."

Isa raised an eyebrow. "Right." Why bother to farm the marshes? Surely this pit was too poor to feed many people. But then, they'd only stuck a few roundhouses here, scraping the muck and pretending that this little place was all the world. Just like everywhere else between here and June. *Disgusting,* Isa thought. Years ago, this was all tributary to Cantium. *Did people travel then?* Isa wondered. *Did they ever go to Cantium?* Isa didn't know, but she guessed that they did; not like these wretches in the mud.

Frog Man was waiting for her to say something, still blinking his buggy eyes. "I'm looking for the kingdom of Cantium," she said. "Have you heard of it? Has anyone you know ever gone near there?"

"Oh, yes, I've been to Cantium," he said.

Isa was already leaning away, ready to escape this

marsh and Frog Man's stench. "Well, anyway. Didn't think so. Just thought I'd ask... Wait. What did you say?"

"I've been to Cantium," Frog Man repeated, speaking slowly as though she were dense. "Many times. I'm popular there."

"You have actually seen Cantium?" Isa asked, her excitement rising. "It isn't lost – it still exists?"

"Of course it exists," said Frog Man. "It's all there."

Isa took a deep breath. "But I mean Cantium, the great hill kingdom," she said. "Where they made the art and sang the songs. It can't be like that any more."

"It's as great as ever," said Frog Man, smiling. "More people and houses than you've ever seen."

Isa couldn't believe it. For so long, her hopes had been sinking, and now... At last, at last! Salvation for the land of June! She wanted to shout with joy, to call to her brother, Tuni: *It's all right! They're coming for you! They'll save you at last.*

She was so excited, she almost didn't hear Frog Man say that Cantium was two days' walk away. Extraordinary, she thought, for it to be so close to this dreadful pit. "Which way do I go?" she asked.

Frog Man regarded her with a look of almost pity. "Don't trouble yourself," he said after a moment. "I'll take you there."

"Really?" Isa asked doubtfully. "You don't have to stay here?"

He smiled. "I'm free as a bird. They're sleeping, you see," he added, gesturing at the roundhouses.

Isa beamed. Frog Man wasn't bad after all. Except for his stench. One would have thought that he'd clear up once away from his native air, but the farther they got from the marsh, the more he seemed to stink. But Isa didn't care. She sang and skipped along, while Frog Man blinked at her and shook his head.

Frog Man's real name was Tach. As they walked, he

told her about Cantium. "They have huge gates and defenses. Like nothing you've ever seen! I thought about doing that for the marsh. Banks and ditches just like on the great hill. I could if I wanted, you know."

"Right," said Isa. He never tired of talking about himself, she thought. Why such a need to impress?

When they stopped at night beside a spring, Isa made him wash his face. Tach blustered and raved, but in the end he obeyed. "Much better," Isa said, satisfied. Tach stuck out his tongue at her. Now she saw that he was a young man in his mid-twenties, about the age of her brother, Batt. He had none of Batt's haughty handsomeness, but he was pleasing enough.

At dusk the next evening, in gathering fog, they emerged from the trees on the last stretch of road to Cantium. "Where is it?" asked Isa. She had expected a soaring hill above the plain.

"There." Tach pointed.

Through the fog, Isa could just see the outline of a hill, long, but almost flat. "It's not very high," she said.

"It just seems that way from down here," Tach said confidently. "Once we're up it, you'll see."

They passed down a long, straight lane through fields where cows lowed in the distance. Cantium must be rich, if they had cattle, Isa thought. In June cows were rare.

As they approached the hill and began to climb, Isa saw what Tach had meant. The hill was immense. It sloped up gradually, sprawling over many acres, seeming small only because the eye could not take it all in. *Yes, it's here!* Isa thought jubilantly. *It's great after all.* She imagined the games, the feasts, the epic song competitions lasting long into the night.

Below them at the base of the hill sat an earthen mound, about ten feet high and twenty feet long. "That's a king's burial," said Tach.

A king! Isa's breath quickened. This was a burial on a

scale she had never seen, right here on the plain amid the mud and the cows. A bird hovered over the mound, wings outstretched in flight, flapping in the wind but going nowhere. The bird was like the king, Isa thought; one who would never truly come down from on high. As long as she looked, and when she turned away and then looked again, the bird was there above the mound, and she thought it might fly there for eternity.

The soil on the mound was fresh, only recently dug. Isa thought of this as they ascended the great banks and ditches that protected the hill. *Cantium! Cantium!* It was still a city, still the seat of a king. *People said it was destroyed, but they were wrong!* And soon vast armies would sweep down to June's aid.

The ditches were man-made canyons, both sides swooping far, far up to the sky. Isa and Tach wound through them, hearing the murmur of voices from up above. Now they were up! Isa strained to see the people, but the fog concealed them. No matter. She'd soon see them all, the great crowd. Closer, closer. And then...

The great shock. Only a few people stood there in the fog, or rather, stooped over the ground, squabbling amongst themselves. They wore dirt-smeared tunics and looked as though they'd never combed their hair. Beyond them was a row of huts, most half-falling down. No one took any notice of Isa and Tach. With growing dread, Isa noticed that their faces were too thin, like they were starving.

"I don't understand," she said, turning to Tach. "Where is Cantium?"

"This *is* Cantium," Tach said proudly. "Isn't it grand? In the marshes, we don't have nearly so many houses."

A cold, sinking feeling gripped Isa's chest. She ran her fingers through her hair. "But what are they doing?" The squabbling seemed to be over small slabs of wood, which some people were dragging away.

"Getting roofs for their houses," said Tach. "It's going

to rain, you see."

Isa took a deep breath. *There are still people here,* she told herself. *I can still ask them for help. I can salvage this somehow.* She swallowed. "Excuse me!" The Cantians kept on fighting over the scraps. "Excuse me!"

Eventually a few stopped and frowned at her, this golden-haired stranger. She cleared her throat. "I am Isa Uli-ac of the land of June."

Some of them went back to picking over scraps. The others stood silently.

"We're under attack from a foreign enemy, the Remi," said Isa, quavering under their stares. "They've decimated our fields and stolen our land."

"Why should we care?" asked a man.

Isa felt herself begin to panic. "June is your ally. You're supposed to protect us."

"June?" said the man. "Never heard of it."

"Of course you haven't heard of it," laughed another. "There's no such place."

These people were useless! "Never mind, then," Isa said. "Where's your king?"

Their eyes nearly popped out of their heads. A few laughed uncertainly. "We haven't had a king in generations," said a bearded man, frowning.

"Yes, of course you have," Isa snapped. "You must have a new one now. Or if you don't, you're about to get one. I saw the fresh burial in the plain."

They stared at her. Then one, a muscular man with red streaks in his brown hair, started laughing – big, boisterous laughs, as the others gaped at him and at Isa. "Fresh!" he hooted. "Oh, yes, it's fresh." From behind him, he reached and pulled out a skull, half-caked in muddy gold, with the neck bones and part of a shoulder still attached by rotten sinews. Isa swallowed quickly to keep from puking.

Brown-and-red-streaks shook the skull. "That's the king!" he said. "We just dug him up, you see. He's an old lout, but we wanted his gold."

Isa turned away, the sting of vomit sharp in her throat.

"Sorry," Tach whispered. "I thought you knew."

FOUR

he rain came heavily now. "If you're staying here, get out of the way," the bearded man said to Tach. "We can spare a little hut for you and your wife. Don't expect it to be nice."

"We're not married," Isa said hurriedly.

"Goodness, no!" cried Tach, greatly offended. "I wouldn't pick a girl like that! I'd get someone much better, with higher status." Isa glared at him.

"Not married?" said Brown-and-red-streaks, grinning. "Then she's fair game!"

"My turn first," another man said jovially. "You get them all."

"Listen," said Isa, disgusted. "Enemies are in the land of June. You have to help us."

"Woo, crazy girl!" said Brown-and-red-streaks. From behind, someone grabbed at Isa's breasts. She whirled, but saw only laughing faces.

An elderly man swatted away the others and shuffled Isa off to a tumbledown hut, which she was to share with other unmarried women. A large hole gaped in its wattle roof. Isa looked at it doubtfully. "Will this hold off the rain?"

"Better than some," said her escort, departing.

Isa clambered inside. To her horror, she saw that half the space was taken up by three pigs and a sheep. In June, what few livestock the people had lived in close proximity, too, but they never came in the houses. These animals were unbearably smelly. The sheep, with its long, knotted fur and horns that curled along its ears and down its neck, was the worst. Its sharp, acrid odor overpowered her. She'd gladly have exchanged it for Tach and his stench from the marshes.

Holding her nose, Isa settled into a corner and studied the other women in the hut, who paid her little notice. There was an old matron whose teeth had succumbed to rot; a pretty, buxom girl a little older than Isa; and a mousy-haired girl who looked about ten. *Where are their families?* Isa wondered. *Why don't they live with their fathers or brothers?*

The buxom girl was chattering loudly to the other two. Isa cleared her throat; she could still taste the vomit in her mouth from seeing the skull. "Could I have some water?" she asked.

"Catch the rain," said the matron, not looking at her. Isa searched around, but could find no bowl.

"Hello," said a voice from the door. "Are you hungry?"

Gratefully, Isa crawled nearer. A hand stretched in, holding a bowl with shreds of meat. Isa took the bowl and peered out at the giver. It was a slender girl, about twelve years old, with straggly hair from the rain. "I'm Seri," said the girl. "Are you from the marshes?"

"No," said Isa as she chewed. "From far away. The land of June."

"June?" Seri wrinkled her nose, which was covered in

freckles. "Sounds nice." She looked further into the hut. "That's my little sister," she said, pointing at the mousy-haired girl. "Her name's Sham. What's your name?"

"Isa."

"Sham, be nice to Isa."

A large figure loomed up behind Seri: the bearded man who had told Isa and Tach to get out of the way. He stared at Isa disdainfully, then put a hand on Seri's shoulder to lead her away. Seri smiled. "Good night, Isa. Sleep well." She stood up in the doorway and walked off with the bearded man.

"Is that her father?" Isa asked.

The buxom girl giggled. "That's Oram, her husband."

Isa stared at her. Seri was so young! This wretched place – this was Cantium?

From Isa's nest in the corner, she could see half the sky. Soon the hole in the roof made her sopping wet from the rain. The others huddled up together on the other side of the hut, somewhat dry, but so close to the animals; Isa couldn't stand the smell. She sang June songs to herself in her head, but sleep wouldn't come.

In the middle of the night, a man stepped in through the hole in the roof. His black form blotted out the stars. He lay behind Isa and kissed her neck, pulling back her hair in the dark. "Stop," said Isa. "Stop!"

"Shh, pretty one," he whispered. "This won't take long."

From his voice, Isa knew that he was the man with red streaks in his hair who had laughed as he showed her the skull. Now she felt his wet hair on her neck. She flung an elbow back against the soft, warm flesh of his belly. "Ow!" he said. "Careful."

She kicked backwards, hard, then rolled and began to scratch him with her nails. "Ow!" he said again, pulling back.

"Hmm? Who's there?" muttered the matron sleepily. The girl, Sham, moaned and turned over, not liking to be woken.

"Go to sleep, little one," the man whispered.

The matron coughed softly. "Get out of here, Jord."

"I can come to you, too, Minsul," he said teasingly. "Don't be jealous." She cursed at him; he laughed.

"Don't forget me," cooed the buxom girl, who was also now awake.

Jord crawled over to her. "You're too sharp, anyway," he told Isa. "Such nails!"

Isa curled up miserably, cold and wet, trying not to listen to the man with the girl. The rain drummed on. She thought of the land of June, of summer dancing, of gentle Tuni laid out on his bed. *Tuni, help me!* she cried silently. *I suffer, too.*

She finally fell asleep, for she awoke to gray morning. The rain had stopped and Jord was gone. The other three were awake and stretched out lazily on their blankets. Isa sat up, groggy from lack of sleep. From the hole in the roof, she could tell it was well past sunrise. What a waste of the day! In June, the people would be far off in the fields. "What can I do to help?" she asked.

"Oh, nothing, nothing," said the matron, Minsul. "There's no hurry."

"But surely there's work," said Isa. "Food to get, or something?"

Minsul waved a hand. "We'll do that later. No hurry."

Isa sat in the hut with them for a few minutes, not wanting to be a rude guest. But she was in Cantium! The men last night had laughed at her, but others might help. *Someone must!* she thought as she clambered out of the hut through the open roof. In the old days, Cantium had protected June. If enemies came, Cantium would have rushed to June's aid.

The rows of roundhouses stretched much farther than Isa had thought when she'd seen them last night in the fog. On and on she walked, and still the rows went on. The hilltop was so vast that there was no single place where she could stand and see from end to end. Many little swells and hills rose in the midst of it. She kept thinking she had reached the end, only to see more hills and rises, more rows of roundhouses. So many people! Probably a couple thousand all together; about equal to June, in a more concentrated space. Not as many as had once lived in Cantium, but enough. If only they'd help!

Here and there people sat in the mud in front of the houses. Stone bowls lay nearby, but no one was grinding grain. Only a few wet twigs stocked the cooking pits, but no one was gathering wood. Everyone sat idly, staring at the ground, or off into the distance, or at Isa as she walked past. All seemed content, with no one in a hurry to move. Isa didn't understand it.

She kept on past the houses, headed for the east "gate": an opening between two mounds of dirt at the edge of the hilltop before it dropped down into the banks and ditches. Anyone could have walked through. As Isa neared the gate, the houses fell away, leaving only open space between her and the edge. Back at the west gate, where she and Tach had entered last night, the houses pressed much closer, and Isa guessed they once had here, too, when Cantium was great.

Suddenly there was a commotion. Three men came in the gate, two of them holding up the other by the armpits. Isa stared at them with horror. All three were bloody, but the one in the middle was the worst, drenched in red from his right shoulder down to his hip. His arm dangled awkwardly like it was held on only by the skin.

Isa felt the bile in her throat. She thought of Tuni being carried back from battle; Tuni with his belly gaping; Tuni wracked with pain. Why did no one watch the gate? "Help!" she yelled toward the houses. "Help!" The wind caught her words; it was so cursed windy up here. Did anyone hear her?

Isa ran forward, then halted in alarm. The man with the worst wound was Jord of the red-streaked hair, who had come to the hut last night. Ugh. But he was in no condition to bother her. He moaned piteously, drooping his head, his face chalk-white from the loss of blood. Isa didn't recognized the two men who helped him.

"Strangers," gasped one of these, a stout man with black hair. "They wore metal. So well-made!"

"The Remi," said Isa. She turned her head, trying not to look at Jord. If she touched the blood or peeled back his tunic, she'd faint.

His two helpers only stared at her. They hadn't been at the west gate last night, so had never seen Isa nor heard of the Remi.

People were coming from the houses now. A small crowd formed. Among them was Tach, who went to stand beside Isa, looking maddeningly well-rested after such a rainy night.

"Ay, Rye, what happened?" someone called.

"They killed two of our men," said the black-haired helper. "We barely got away."

"What were you doing down there?" Tach asked. Isa was grateful that he was near her, because he could catch her if she passed out. Jord's arm was still just hanging there, swinging, swinging...

"We were hunting for deer on the plain," said the other helper, a tall man. "Lucky we had these." He held up a sheath of hunting knives. Isa staggered and gripped Tach's arm. The weapons were sticky with gore, dripping chunks of flesh – and Isa had a hunch it wasn't animal flesh.

"They were so smart," said Rye, the black-haired one. He was fiddling with a trinket he wore around his neck, wiping the blood from it as he smoothed his tunic. "Outwitted us. And we weren't being dumb, either. Tell 'em, Fells."

"They figured us out so fast," said the tall helper, Fells. "They shouldn't have realized what we were doing, looping around the fields to trick them. But they did."

"A pretty story," said someone in the crowd. "Likely you got jumped by some shepherds."

"No!" Rye said, protesting. "Their weapons were so much better than ours. Uncanny. They killed Lannon with this one." He waved a long, slender sword. "Just look at it. Light and strong at the same time. I wonder how they made it." Isa grimaced: it was Remi steel.

"Fool," said Fells. "Why didn't you leave it? Then you'd have had less to carry when we were trying to get Jord away."

"Aw, I had to keep it," said Rye. "Look at it shine against my clothes."

"It's the Remi who attacked you," Isa broke in. "They're naturally smart. Inhuman. We have to fight them."

"Get out of the way, girl," someone said.

Men were lifting Jord by the arms and legs, carrying him toward the houses. Everyone else was melting away. *So they're going to do nothing?* Isa thought. Tach still stood near her, so she grabbed him by the arm. "Ow!" he said.

"You have to call a council," Isa said. "It's urgent."

"I can't!" said Tach, trying to wriggle away. "I'm not Cantian. Besides, I don't think they have councils."

He winced as she dug in her fingernails. "You have to call one," she said. "The Remi are here! We're all in danger."

"Fine, fine," he said, and she released him. "I don't see why you can't call one yourself," he muttered, rubbing his arm.

"Women can't call councils," Isa said. "At least, they can't in June."

"I'm sure no one will care," said Tach.

He was right. At first Isa merely walked with him, telling him what to say, but soon she saw that the Cantians listened as well to her as to Tach. Odd; but then, the Cantians didn't seem to care about anything, so why would they care that she was female? Now she and Tach could work twice as fast. While she canvassed one row of roundhouses, she sent him off down another so she wouldn't have to hear his incessant self-praise. "A pity you've lost so many teeth," he was saying to a man as she walked away. "No one in the marshes has lost more than five, thanks to me. Why don't I cook you up some barley hash? Nice and soft, so it doesn't hurt your gums."

Despite Isa's and Tach's efforts, the sun was high before the council met. Isa would hardly have called it a council. Anyone who wanted to come, came, even women and a pair of six-year-old twin boys. Apart from them, Isa had seen few children in Cantium. Disease, she guessed, or lack of nourishment. In June, children were abundant, although not all made it there, either: of Aunt and Uncle's six, only little Denn remained. "We should start the meeting," she said.

"Not yet," said Fells, the tall man who had helped Jord this morning. "Wait for more people."

Isa clenched her hands. Though it was sunny, she shivered; a strong wind blew up from the plain. A few more people trickled in: the matron, Minsul, from Isa's tent, as well as the buxom girl and ten-year-old Sham; the stout man, Rye, with his captured Remi sword. He swung this trophy with a flourish, making the buxom girl laugh. "Ay, Thistle!" Rye said to her. "Look at this. Gorgeous, isn't it?"

"Yes." Thistle giggled. "If you think a sword can be gorgeous." She tossed her hair.

Isa shifted impatiently. "We need to start."

"They're coming, they're coming," said Fells. "Wait a little more." He stretched out on the ground and flopped his arm over his face to shield his eyes from the sun.

And so Isa waited, while the land of June was dying. *I came to ask their help,* she thought. *But they won't act on their own. It's up to me.*

FIVE

*H*er waiting was useless, for only two more people came: the girl, Seri, who had brought Isa food last night, and her middle-aged husband, Oram, who scowled at Isa. "You again?" he said. "We've had enough trouble."

The council numbered twenty or so, out of all Cantium's hundreds. Isa explained again about the Remi, their uncanny talents, and their battle with June, with an added description of the attack on Jord's men this morning.

"Now the Remi are at your door," she said. "If you don't act, you'll be conquered like we were."

Oram fixed his eyes on her. "You know nothing. We are many. There are only four of these Remi."

Rye laughed. "Three of them, now." He spun the Remi sword around in his hand. "He didn't know what hit him. Turned his head, and boom, I was there."

"You weren't so cheerful this morning, when your friends were killed," Isa snapped. "Bet you didn't brag to them."

Rye had nothing to say to that. Oram glowered at Isa.

"What do you propose?" asked Minsul. She was sitting cross-legged, repairing broken reeds on an old basket. Isa hadn't thought she'd been listening.

"Where there are three Remi, there are many more," said Isa. "They must have a camp near here. You can't wait for them to get settled. Then it'll be too late." She looked around for friendly faces, but saw none. *Why don't they understand?* "We need to strike at them now. Mount an attack. They expect us to stay here on the hill, so they won't be prepared."

Fells yawned from where he lay on the ground. "So much effort, for an uncertain result. Just leave them down there on the plain."

"Yes, leave them down there," Minsul agreed. "Don't bother them, and they won't hurt us."

"They already have," Isa said, exasperated. "Will you please sit down?!"

Rye was prancing around with his Remi sword, flourishing fake passes at the six-year old twin boys, which set them off giggling. He made a face at Isa and remained standing.

"You have no right to judge us," said Oram. "We know Cantium, and you do not."

Seri piped up from beside him. "I think she means that they've already hurt us, with our men killed and wounded."

Isa's heart swelled for this little girl, this twelve-year-old bride. Her husband glowered. "You're a fool," Oram said to Isa. "Go back to where you came from."

"Please," Isa said. "We have an old alliance. You must help us! Cantium and June are friends."

Fells shrugged. "I don't see why we should do all that for a place we haven't even heard of."

"Come now," said Isa. "Someone here must have heard of it." Silence. "Anyone? Please tell me you've heard of the land of June." More silence. Her eyes searched the crowd and found Seri, who looked like she wanted to agree. "Have you?"

The girl gazed at Isa, mouth quivering. "No," she said, and looked away. Oram smirked with triumph, and the council closed. The Cantians would do nothing.

"What now?" Tach asked in a low voice.

Isa took in a breath. "There's one other person we can try."

Jord's hut was worse than the one Isa had slept in; it had no roof at all. He was laid out in the corner upon a nest of reeds: a ratty, sodden pile, not clean like Isa had made Tuni's bed. Now she covered her nose at the rancid odor as she and Tach stepped inside.

Jord grinned at her. "Come to my bed, pretty thing?"

Isa was about to pass out from the sight of him. He was bare to the waist, with bandages clumped around his right shoulder. The cloths were filthy and flies buzzed around the wound. His bloody tunic, which someone had cut away, lay in a heap beside him.

"Listen," she snapped. "No one here will listen. Where there's one Remi, there's more. Lots more. They're strong, smart, and we can't compete with them."

"I believe you," said Jord.

Oh. That was easy. Isa let out a breath. "Really?"

"I saw how they fought our men." He shrugged with his good shoulder. "They're clearly dangerous."

Isa looked away so she didn't have to see those bandages. "Cantium must fight the Remi," she said. "Now, before they come up the hill and conquer you." *I'll hold off on telling them to go to June,* she thought. Yes, that was her end goal, but the Cantians were more likely to move if they saw themselves under threat. They were selfish, like all people.

Jord lifted his good arm and coughed into his hand.

"First we have to see how many there are, where they're set up. Someone has to go down and spy on them." He regarded Tach, who stood blinking at him with his frog eyes. "You," said Jord. "What's your name? You can be our scout."

Tach's eyes widened. "Oh, no," he said hurriedly. "You wouldn't want that. I'm, ah, of better use up here."

Jord sneered. "Coward, are you? Well, that's no surprise. You're from the marshes."

Tach reared up angrily. "The people of the marshes are far better than you! They look to me as their leader. That's why I can't risk spying on the Remi. Without me..."

"I will go," said Isa, interrupting.

Jord waved his hand dismissively. "You're a woman."

"You don't understand," said Isa. "I've seen the Remi. I know how they work. One of you might see their houses, but you couldn't guess from that what they're trying to do."

Jord shrugged. "Go, then. But you'll need a Cantian to guide you." He grinned. "And to enjoy your pretty face."

Isa fought the urge to slap him. In a moment, she'd be out of the hut and rid of him. He might be dead soon, but she didn't care. "Can I take a message from you to the others? If it's you asking instead of me, maybe someone will agree to go."

"No, no. I'll go myself," said Jord. He flung his legs off the bed and stood.

Isa gaped at him. "But your arm!"

Jord glanced down at it, hanging uselessly beneath its crust of bandages. He tucked his hand into the side of his trousers, so the arm couldn't flop around. "There," he said cheerfully. "Now we'll be on our way." And he strode out the door.

Thus Isa learned that not all Remi wounds were as dire as her brother Tuni's. How unfair, she thought as she grabbed Tach to make him follow, that her good, gentle brother got the hard cut and this brute of a Jord got the light.

The descent from Cantium was a walk fit for a king.

The ramparts rose out of each other, equal in size and magnitude. In places, hunters and other travelers had worn paths down through the banks and ditches. When Isa, Jord, and Tach finally emerged from the last rampart, the steep base of the hill was yet below them, sweeping down into the fields. *It's a different world down here*, Isa thought. People seemed smaller, more vulnerable. No wonder the Cantians of old went up the hill to dream.

"All this nice farmland," Isa said as they walked. "Why do you waste it?"

"We farm it," Jord said defensively. "A few of us live down here permanently, to tend the crops."

"No wonder you Cantians are starving!" Isa exclaimed. "You need far more people down here. Not just..."

"Hmm," said Jord. "That's odd."

Isa stopped alongside him. "What?"

"The Cantian farmers. One of them lived right here. But where is the house?" Jord pointed at the ground. A raised circle, bare of grass, marked the spot where a roundhouse had been. No other traces remained.

Isa ground her teeth angrily. "The Remi."

"I don't like this," Tach moaned.

Jord frowned. "Be careful," he said. "We'll go on, but quietly."

He steered them clear of the copse where the Remi party had attacked his men. Further on, a river wound across the plain, much bigger than the June river where little Denn had first seen the Remi. "Careful," said Jord. "There's not much cover here, except for the grass. We'll have to crouch low so they don't see us."

"Where's Tach?" Isa asked suddenly.

Jord looked around. "Damned if I know. He was here a minute ago."

"The Remi must have got him," Isa said, slumping. "Poor Tach! It's my fault for making him come."

"Don't be silly," said Jord. "How could the Remi have

gotten him, when we're right here and didn't see a thing? That's one advantage of this open space. We'll see them coming, sure as they see us." He moved forward. "Let's go. Maybe Tach will turn up. We can't stand around here waiting for him, when there isn't any cover."

The Remi camp lay on the plain near the river. It was smaller than Bridge Town, holding only forty men by Isa's count. Perhaps they were advance scouts, come to mark out future settlements. Isa hated that idea. "They already have June," she hissed in Jord's ear. "Why come all the way to Cantium?"

"Maybe there are a great many of them," Jord whispered back. "Enough that they have to spread out from here to your June, and settle all the lands in between." Isa shuddered; gods forbid. "But look at that," Jord added. "Those men there, with the Remi. They're our farmers! I see Haffer, and Nax, and Garley. They're all there."

"The one whose house was gone?" Isa asked.

Jord looked. "He's there, too."

Isa sighed. "At least the Remi haven't killed them. But now they're slaves." She turned away. It was happening again: an old land conquered, its people left to despair.

Jord shook his head. "I don't think so. Look, they're smiling and laughing. If they're slaves, they're darned cheerful ones."

Isa looked again. He was right; none of the Cantian farmers looked distressed. "But why?" she asked, puzzled. "Don't they fear the Remi?"

Jord shrugged. "I suppose they've gone over to their side."

"Well, that's rich of them," Isa said indignantly. "By now, they'll have told the Remi your weaknesses. Only so long before they storm the Cantium hill."

"*I'm* ready for them," Jord declared. "You should see me fight, girl. Let me against the Remi, and you won't be so quick to turn me from your bed."

Once again, it took an effort not to slap him. "Idiot," Isa hissed. "Your arm's hanging by a thread from the last time you met them. Or have you forgotten?" She scanned the camp. The Remi wouldn't just sit idle with the Cantian farmers. Somewhere there had to be a sign of their intelligence, an inkling of their plans. Ah, there: a pile of rocks on the riverbank. "See what they're doing?" she said, pointing. "They're damming up the river."

Jord sucked in his breath. "More than that," he said sharply. "They're cutting off the water supply to Cantium!"

Isa stared at him. "How can this be your water supply? It's so far from the hill!"

"Yes, but the copse is the closest the river comes. We cart it up. Damn the bastards!" Jord ran his fingers through his hair. "If the river doesn't flow to the copse, and they control it here, we'll have no access to it."

"Is there any other place?" Isa asked.

"There's a small pond on the other side of the hill, but the water's brackish." Jord tucked in his wounded arm and straightened to a crouch, so that the tall grass still hid him from the Remi. "This is going to be a problem."

Once they were out of view of the camp and past the copse, Tach finally reappeared. "Oh, hello," he said nonchalantly. "Going back up, then?"

"Where were you?" demanded Isa. "We were worried."

"Just wandering," said Tach, gesturing vaguely to the east. "I climbed that hill over there. Nice view."

"Did you, now?" Jord crossed his good arm over the injured one. "That's strange. Takes half a day to walk there and back. Where'd you get the time?"

Tach's eyes widened. "Oh, no, no," he said hurriedly. "Actually I was napping just over there, by the trees."

Jord raised an eyebrow. "Napping? Quite different from climbing, like you said first."

"He's here now," Isa said impatiently. "Let's go. We have to tell the people on the hill about the Remi."

"Watch that one," Jord murmured as they walked back to the Cantium hill. Tach was ahead of them, slapping at the grass with a stick he'd picked up and humming something out of tune.

"He's from the marshes," said Isa. "A little weird in the head, but harmless."

Jord raised his eyebrows, but said nothing more.

SIX

*B*ack on the hill, Isa remembered why she was so frustrated with Cantium. "Excuse me," she said to some people who still sat idly by their huts, though by now it was mid-afternoon. "I need to call a council." The people sat and blinked at her.

"Dear Isa." Jord grinned and hugged her shoulders; she pushed him away. "So civil," he said, sneering at her. "But really, you go about it the wrong way. Allow me." He strode down the path between the houses. "Our water's gone!" he bellowed. "Our water's gone! Our water's gone!"

Isa glared at his back. He could have warned her before splitting her ears. But his shouting worked. Already more heads were popping out of the roundhouses, voices were calling out questions. Jord marched away without answering them, leaving the people to follow.

Once Jord and Isa explained about the dam, all the Cantians, even surly Oram, believed in the danger. "We have very little time," said Fells, the tall man. "We only have the pond to drink. Two or three weeks, at most, before we start to get sick from that water."

"Or even less," said Minsul. "My husband died from drinking there." Isa had wondered why Minsul lived with the younger girls.

Black-haired Rye slammed a hand down on his thigh. "Let's go right down and root them out. We have weapons. Let's do it now!"

"You can't just grab some swords and fight the Remi," said Isa. "They'd annihilate you! I saw it in June. Wait a bit. Take some time to train your army."

"No need," said Oram. He sat with his little wife, Seri, who looked at him reverently as he spoke. "It'll just be a skirmish. We don't need to train."

"It will be bigger than a skirmish," Isa said. Now was her chance to pull these Cantians up out of the muck, to make them remember what they once had been. "Think of it. Finally, something worthy of your time! A grand battle like those of your ancestors. Cantium will rise again! But you have to wait, prepare yourselves. Rush in, and they will destroy you."

"All right," Fells said, laughing. "It's easier if we don't have to fight right now."

To Isa's relief, most of the men seemed to heed her argument. "Yes, prepare for battle!" Rye exclaimed. "Then we'll get the devils."

As the people disbanded for the night, Isa felt heartened. Now the Cantians would surely move. But in the morning, nothing happened.

"Let's get to work," Isa said. "We need piles of weapons. Stronger defenses. Practice sessions for the army."

"Working on it," said Fells. But he wasn't. No one was. Two days ticked by as Isa pulled her hair in frustration.

"I don't see how Cantium was ever great," she said angrily. She was sitting with Jord and Tach at the east gate, staring down in the direction of the Remi camp. "You're all lazy and useless. Your very lives are threatened, and you don't even care!"

"We're not like your June," said Jord. "People aren't used to working together. We need hierarchy. Someone commanding us to get things done. That's why we had kings."

"In the marshes we don't need kings," said Tach. At least, that's what it sounded like; he had found a rotten apple somewhere and was stuffing it into his mouth.

Disgusting, Isa thought, watching him. Tach may have washed his face, but he was still from that vile marsh. "Fine," she said. "We'll get a king to lead us, if that's what it takes to make people move."

"Minor problem," said Jord, picking at his bandaged arm. "The last king's dead in the ground, and has been for ages."

"Yes, I remember." Isa shuddered. If Jord hadn't held up that putrefied skull the first night she was here, she might have thought better of Cantium. "We can make someone the king."

Jord laughed. "Right. But who?" He ticked off people on his fingers. "Oram's a crotchety old devil. He'd rule with an eye to his own good, not Cantium's. Fells is a fine guy, but he's lazy. Rye is childish. And there's no one else of note."

What about you? Isa thought. But she didn't trust Jord, and she wasn't going to put the idea in his head if he hadn't thought of it already. "We'll elect someone," she said aloud. "Whoever we all choose will have to do."

"We can't elect a king," Jord said patiently. "It never worked like that. It was whoever was strongest, whoever could take charge."

Tach said something else about how they did things in the marshes. Isa didn't listen. She was sick of waiting, sick of all these words swirling around without anyone ever acting. "I'll do it," she said. "I'll be the king."

Tach choked on his apple.

Jord grinned widely. "Well, there's an idea."

Isa was already on her feet. That same hour, she called a meeting of the Cantians, where she was not warmly received.

"I will not serve under a woman," Oram declared.

"Nor I," said another. Several of the men were nodding their heads.

"Come now," said Jord. "It won't be so bad. How can you say no to my pretty Isa?"

"Not *your* Isa," she said.

Jord laughed. "It's not like it would be new," he told the crowd. "What of the earth goddess? The sun, the moon, and the stars? They're female and no one makes a stink about them."

"Yes, that's true," Fells said slowly. "A woman could have power, I suppose."

"What's this, then?" Oram demanded. "A stranger comes here one day, and the next, she makes herself our king? We can fend for ourselves, thank you."

"I don't *want* to be king," Isa snapped. "But someone's got to. Just like someone had to leave June to come to Cantium. That will all be a waste, unless you get off your butts and listen to me."

Rye broke into a broad grin. "Ha! A fine joke. Come on, let her be king! This will be more fun than we've had in years."

"Let her! Let her!" people chanted.

Isa was surprised at how easily they proclaimed her king, with no debate after Oram's first protests. As if they didn't care who led them, or if they were led at all. *Only in stupid, lazy, useless Cantium,* she thought, *would a strange girl be able to walk in and proclaim herself king.* Let them think that it was a joke, if that got them moving. She, Isa, would make her plans and take the Cantians further than they'd ever dreamed.

"Right," she said, drawing herself up tall, as she imagined a king would stand. "Time for action. Gather all the weapons that you have and meet back here. We'll have to take stock of our supplies and start our training program. We'll have to make sure we spread out the arms as evenly as we can so that everyone has at least one weapon. Then we'll... Hello?"

People were talking amongst themselves, some strolling away, others idling about and gazing at Isa.

"Why won't they listen to me?" she said angrily, swinging around to face Jord. "I'm the king, aren't I? You said they would listen. Or were you lying?"

Jord smirked at her. "You can't just become king. You have to have the trappings first. Look, they're finding some for you."

People were stirring now, excited, swarming in and out of the roundhouses with an air of importance. Someone pressed a sword into Isa's hand. It was heavier than she expected and she almost dropped it. "Careful," Jord said. "That's a fine piece of work."

Isa examined the iron hilt. It was beautifully decorated, with hundreds of tiny circles pressed into the metal. "Why would you let such a nice thing just lie around in someone's house?" she said irritably.

Jord shrugged. "Why not? We've had nothing better to do with it."

Old Minsul approached with a slender strap woven from light brown reeds. "A token of divinity," she said, tying the strap around Isa's forehead. "Be one with the world, King Isa," she intoned. "One with the gods. One with the waters. Live for us all, and bring the wholeness."

Isa huffed impatiently. "Can we get started? The Remi are waiting."

"A ring!" Fells said. "Does anyone have a ring?"

"Rye has a ring," someone said.

Rye turned pale beneath his black hair. "Oh, please, let me keep it!" he begged. "It's got little carvings on it. This is the nicest thing I have. Get a ring from someone else."

"It's a good ring," said Fells, plucking it unceremoniously from Rye's hand. "Fit for a king." He slid it onto Isa's finger. Rye glared at Isa, and she had the uncomfortable feeling that she had made a new enemy; as if she needed another, after Oram.

Jord's breath was warm in her ear. "Last of all," he murmured. "Gold from the last king's grave." He slipped a bracelet around her wrist. Like the sword, it burst with ornate designs.

Isa gagged. "Don't make me wear that." Probably the bracelet still smelled of musty, decaying flesh.

"A king needs a bracelet," Jord said. "And this one won't kill you."

"The king! The king!" people chanted.

"Call me a queen, at least," Isa grumbled to Jord.

"Won't do," said Jord, patting her cheek. "The war leaders of Cantium have always been kings. If we called you queen, there'd be a whole new set of expectations: baking bread, blessing the hearths, overseeing the potter girls." He grinned impishly. "Would you like that better?"

"I'll be a king, thank you," Isa said icily.

Now that people knew how to react to her, with her recognizable title, Isa could finally act. The Cantians had a surprising number of weapons cached around the hill. Not to the former extent, surely, but there were ample remnants of Cantium's former power. Rye, for instance, stowed the sword of some great-great-grandfather under his bed when he wasn't using it for cutting cheese. Fells had a heap of rusted weapons piled beside his door. No reason, really, but why get rid of them? Many people were like that. By the time Isa and her helpers finished their rounds, they had enough iron to outfit their army several times over.

Isa had never held a sword. How was she to lead the training sessions? She stood before the men, nervous and shivering from the cold. Oram caught her eye, and she saw that he knew she didn't know what to do. He opened his mouth to speak, but Jord got there before him.

"Listen up!" Jord said briskly. "Isa's asked me to be her agent for the training. You lot, stand over there. The rest of you, over there. We'll start with sword exercises."

Isa bristled. She'd asked nothing of Jord. *Be careful,* she told herself. *He wants to take power for himself. That's why he supported me as king.* Maybe he had thought the people wouldn't accept him as their leader, so he had to weasel his way in with other methods.

Jord was a good leader, though. He demonstrated the sword techniques with his left hand, since his right arm was still injured from the Remi attack. Soon, he had the session in full swing and Isa discreetly slipped into the first row so that she could learn, too.

SEVEN

*T*hat first day, Isa got cold in spite of the exertion. It was so exposed up here on the height. Even now, not so far out of summer, the wind swooped up and chilled her bones.

"You're blue as a riverfish," Minsul said after the training.

Isa hugged herself closer. "It's freezing."

Minsul look at her appraisingly. "You need real clothes. None of this thin little dress. Come."

In the half-fallen shack where Isa had slept, Minsul took out a fur cape made of sheepskin, a red woolen tunic, and thick trousers. "Normally, you'd have a wool skirt," said Minsul. "But you'd better take these if you're to train with the men."

"Thank you," Isa said gratefully. Some Cantians, at least, weren't so bad after all.

It got better after that, with the warm clothes. Isa and the Cantians trained four times a day, with breaks for meals and cleaning weapons. Though the sword was still heavy in her hand, Isa found that swinging it was much like swinging a scythe, and she was strong enough. Some of the men complained, though.

"I don't see why we have to do all this," Oram snapped. His forehead gleamed with sweat.

"Quit your grumbling!" Jord said, raising his sword. "Come, do a pass with me. Not like that, Fells," he added.

"I'm doing it," Fells said lazily.

"Not very well," said Jord. "Watch." He swung his sword above his right shoulder, then down to his left hip, then up again above his left shoulder, and down again to his right hip.

"Now?" Fells tried to do the move in a quick flourish, not wanting to expend much effort.

"No," Jord said. He glanced on down the row. "Nice job, Rye. Yes, that's right."

"How do you know so much about sword fighting?" Isa asked him.

"My father taught me," said Jord, eyeing Oram as he huffed and grunted through the sword exercises. "Da loved the old stories of Cantium. He wanted that grand warrior life." In a sudden movement, Jord swung out his hand and rapped Oram lightly on the biceps. Oram cursed and dropped his sword. "Hold it firmly!" Jord said. "You've got to be ready for someone to unman you. And then there's the raiding," he continued to Isa, as if in the same stream of conversation. "The boys and I are always out looking for treasure and harrying the swamp people. I like to be in shape for that."

Isa frowned. "You raid the swamp people?"

Jord's laugh rang in the crisp fall air. "Doesn't ol' Tach ever tell you about that? Although in his version, he's the hero of his people, holding off fifty Cantians all by himself."

"Hmph," Isa said. She hated when Jord made fun of Tach.

Now Jord stood behind her and grasped her by the waist. "You're so beautiful," he whispered.

"Get away," Isa snapped, pushing against him. "I need to take stock of the hill." Jord moved to come with her, but she waved him back angrily.

That afternoon, she walked all around Cantium, familiarizing herself with the gates, the ramparts, and the hidden spaces of the hilltop. There were many houses, true, but also vast expanses left bare. *So much potential for future building,* Isa thought, then reminded herself that she would be here only a short time. *Leave the improvement projects to some future king.* As she circled the hill, she was pleased to discover that the Cantians had heaps of grain stored in various underground chambers. They might need these extra supplies, if the Remi were able to surround the hill.

"Why does no one guard the gates?" she asked Jord when she returned to the training ground.

"No need," he said, tucking his sword in its leather sheath. "Cantium's so big. It takes time and effort to get up our hill."

"Yes," said Isa. "But anyone can walk it. When Tach and I came, we just walked through the ramparts and in the gate. There was no one to stop us."

Jord shrugged. "No one comes here. The people of the plains don't wander."

Yes, Isa had seen that. In her journey to Cantium, she had seen no evidence of trade or large gatherings of people. "But the world is different now," she said. "The Remi are in it."

She stationed guards at both gates and along the maze of the ramparts, where they could call out if they discovered intruders. The set-up worked well, until Rye began to complain. "I want to do something!" he said, pulling at his black hair and looking at Isa plaintively. "None of this sitting around. I need action, or I go mad."

No wonder he was out hunting the day Jord was hurt, Isa thought. *Not idling up here like the rest of these laggards.* She put him in charge of gathering little stones to heap at the gates, which the Cantians, if pressed, could fling down at the enemy. Now Rye was happy. All of the Cantians, actually, seemed more energized. They no longer sat in front of their houses, staring vacantly into the distance – or if they did, they at least spent less time doing it. Those who weren't active participants in the sword training were forever coming to watch it, or helping to fetch lunch and supplies for the warriors.

Isa paced the edge of the hill, searching for weaknesses. It seemed that she had been walking for a long time, cold in the wind but unable to escape from it. Not even the great ditches of this greatest hill could provide shelter when the wind came seeking. Besides that, Isa's feet were wet from the grass. Her knee ached, too, from a hard whack she had taken in training. She walked onward, thinking of nothing but her desire for shelter. She was not unhappy, but she felt no rapture, either, no appreciation for this sublime place.

Then, with a sudden start, she thought of where she was: Cantium, great Cantium, seat of all the stories. These trenches below her were the work of men, her own kind, built an untold time ago. She smiled suddenly. Lifting her face to the wind, she ran a few paces, laughing, elated with the knowledge that she was different from the wind and could play. It was fine to be human; it was beautiful, glorious. *And I'll never be like the Remi,* she thought.

Isa paused to look at the land spread out below the hill – *her* land, she realized with a jolt of pleasure. For she was king of Cantium! *If my brothers could see me now,* she thought. She breathed quickly, invigorated with the idea. King of Cantium; lord of all these plains!

"Isa," said Tach behind her. She jumped in surprise, embarrassed for her thoughts. "You should know," Tach said. "Some of the men are whispering. They think you're driving too hard. They're threatening to quit if they don't get a longer rest today."

"Thank you," Isa said, grateful that he'd made no comment about her daydreaming. Faithful Tach; always helping her. She studied him as they walked back to the training ground. The Cantians had gotten him into clean clothes, so nothing remained of the repulsion from the marsh. Isa decided that she would trust his information and give the fighters extra rest.

"I miss my brother," she said suddenly.

"Hmm?" said Tach. He was staring off into the distance, slowing his steps to fall behind her.

"My brother, Tuni," said Isa. "I never told you about him. He's the reason I came to Cantium. I love him so much." She told Tach about Tuni's warm smile; little Denn's playfulness; Batt's impatience. It was a relief to talk of her family instead of the big fall-of-June story that she told in speeches.

Tach listened quietly, his head cocked to one side. "Don't fear," he said when she was finished. "You'll see your brother soon."

Isa sighed. "If only I could be sure." She passed a hand over her forehead. "At night, I dream that he's dead; gone before I could get back to him. Does he long for me? Maybe he knows that he'll never see me again."

Tach squeezed her shoulder. "Don't torture yourself," he said. "It's like living in the swamps. No use staring at the mud and grime around you. Look up, at the light."

Isa smiled at him, wiping her eyes. All along, to hear him talk, she had thought that Tach liked living in the muck. She glanced at the sun. "It's time to train again. Are you coming?"

Tach blinked. "Oh, I think I'll just stay here," he said quickly. "Take a little walk, maybe."

"All right," said Isa. "See you later."

As she was moving away, Jord came up to walk beside her. "What were you two talking about?" he asked.

"Nothing," Isa said.

Jord looked down at her, frowning. The sun flashed on the red in his hair. "You sure?" he said. "Something's bothering you. Maybe I can help."

"I doubt it," said Isa. She turned to the training ground before he could say more, although she heard his feet crunching behind her.

Some soldiers were clustered around the pile of spears, talking amongst themselves. "...always pushing us so hard," Rye was saying. He stopped abruptly when Isa walked up.

"Hello," she said, smiling. "Are the spears ready?"

"Oh, aye," said one of them. "Reckon they're sturdy, with those extra lashes around the tips."

The men moved to start their sword session. Isa knew they had been grumbling about her; their faces looked dark. Luckily Tach had warned her of this before it got any worse.

"Problem, Rye?" Jord said behind her.

Rye scowled. "No."

"Glad to hear it," Jord said coldly. "Say, why don't we take a walk? You can show me what you're doing with the watch posts."

Rye hesitated. "Haven't you already seen them? Besides, training's about to start. I've got to..."

"*Now,* Rye." Jord grabbed the stout man's arm and pulled him along. Rye looked nervous as they walked away.

Isa stared after them, her fists clenched. What was Jord saying to Rye, leaning in so close to him like that? Isa's breath quickened. Maybe Jord was forming an alliance against her, promising Rye power in the future if only he would pretend to tolerate her a little longer. She must stay on her guard.

Jord returned a few minutes later, looking smug. Isa couldn't stand the sight of him. Fighting her anger, she said, "You didn't need to do that. Tach already told me they're unhappy. I'm going to give them extra time off today."

"Well, I talked to Rye," Jord said, pleased with himself. "He'll obey now."

"But you didn't have to do it so roughly!" Isa cried. Several men turned their heads. Lowering her voice, she said, "Now you've bungled it up. You've made him even more against me."

"I haven't!" Jord protested. "Rye only talks big. The trick is to control his talk, so he doesn't infect the men."

Isa wanted to hit him. Instead, she turned to the circle where the swordsmen were practicing, meaning to give a heartening speech. "Only a little while more," she said loudly, drawing herself up tall. "Soon we'll march on the Remi. We'll be strong! It will be like Cantium of old, when... Hello? Are you listening?"

Everyone had turned to watch Isa's buxom housemate, Thistle, pad up to the training area, her bare feet flapping on the ground. She wore a tight blue dress, in spite of the cold – though Isa saw that beneath it she had thick trousers like the rest of them. Thistle smiled coyly. "Such hard training," she said, her voice lilting. "Don't you ever get tired?"

"All the time," said Fells. "Until we look at you."

Thistle laughed and draped her cloak over her head, pretending to hide from him.

Isa hated Thistle. She was like the girls in June who fawned over Tuni, smoothing their hair and inching up their dresses in the hopes that he would look at them. But Tuni was noble and never took the bait. Thistle's ploys usually worked, and she seemed to delight in distracting the men from their training. More than that, Isa suspected that Thistle talked about her behind her back, helping to feed the men's discontent. Just yesterday it had gotten out that Isa refused to smear goat dung on the walls at night for ritual protection, a Cantian custom, and instead placed a bowl near the door as was done in June. Only someone who shared Isa's round-house could have told them that, and Isa doubted that it had been Minsul or Sham. Now people whispered that she was too foreign to be king of Cantium.

"Get out of the way, Thistle," Jord said. "We're trying to train."

Thistle pouted, twirling the end of her braid around her finger. "I'm not in the way. I want to watch." She reached for Jord, trying to hang on him as he walked.

"Ouch!" he yelped. She had touched his wounded arm.

"I'm sorry!" Thistle cried. "Oh, dear Jord, I'm sorry!"

Jord shifted his arm within its binding. "Never mind. Isa, have we enough spears? Fells says we have only four dozen of them."

Isa sighed. "I know, but it will have to do. There isn't time to make more."

Thistle inched up to Jord, taking care not to brush against him. "You're looking awfully handsome today," she said.

"Thank you," Jord said absently. "Isa, if we don't have enough spears, we'll have to fight the Remi at close range."

"And to watch you with the men!" Thistle said loudly, her cheeks flushed. "You're the strongest, by far, and so quick with the sword."

"We'd do well with just swords," Jord went on, as if Thistle weren't there. "But it would be better to have both."

"Having some spears is better than having none, I suppose," said Isa.

Jord grinned at her. "But you must have the best, my beauty."

Thistle smoothed the front of her dress. "Well," she said testily, turning away. "I see I'm not wanted here."

If only Jord would flirt with Thistle! Isa could have screamed. The one person she wanted Thistle to distract was always at her own elbow, pestering her.

"Here, Isa," said Seri, appearing with a basket. "Have some rye cakes."

"Thank you," Isa said gratefully. She hadn't had a bite

to eat since sunrise. She reached into the basket.

Oram strode up. "A waste on her," he said, gesturing at the food. "You think she's going to be cutting down those Remi, when the time comes? No; it'll be us men. We're the ones who need to build our strength."

"Oh, but husband, she's been working so hard," Seri said, smiling up at him. "There'll be enough to go around, you'll see."

"Hmph," said Oram. He leaned down to let Seri kiss his cheek.

How odd, Isa thought, watching them. Seri was the only person Oram obeyed. He was perpetually grumpy, but seemed to see Seri as fragile and sweet. Oram, in love? *Impossible,* Isa thought. But something in his mind allowed Seri to sway him when no other could.

Jord came near again. "Marry me, Isa," he said softly.

"Ick," said Isa. "Just think, I could share you with Thistle, like you wanted that first night I was here."

"I'm done with that," Jord protested. "My eyes are only for you!"

"Right," said Isa. Maybe tomorrow she'd wake and find that Jord had taken over Cantium. "I'd only marry a man of June," she told him, forgetting her distaste for Nuler, the potter. "They're strong and stoic; never showy like you. They can work all day in the sun. It's always sunny in June."

"Oh, yes, the ideal home," Jord said sarcastically. "And now you're stuck in rainy, windy Cantium. Forgive me for trying to give you warmth."

Isa clenched her teeth and prepared to fling an insult at him.

"Isa," Seri said behind them.

Isa turned. The girl had dropped her snack basket and stood doubled over, clutching her stomach. "Seri!" Isa exclaimed. "What's the matter?"

"The pain!" Seri gasped. "I can't take it any longer."

Isa took her hand and helped her sit on the ground.

"Was it something you ate? How long have you had the pain?"

"Since yesterday," Seri moaned.

Suddenly Oram was upon them, ripping Isa's hand away from Seri's. "Now look what you've done," he growled. "You've made her sick. I told her she shouldn't help around here."

"I haven't done anything," Isa said, exasperated. "If you had half your wits, you'd see that."

"This is what comes of having a woman king," Oram said. "The world's turned on end! We've had nothing but bad luck since you came."

"My stomach," Seri said weakly.

"We'll have to get her inside," Jord said. He knelt beside Seri. "Can you walk?" he asked gently.

"Just stay away from her," Oram barked. He stooped, swept Seri into his arms like she was a sack of grain, then strode off with her over his shoulder.

Isa wanted to run and tear Seri from Oram's arms. "What's he doing?" she cried. "He has to let us take care of her."

"It will be all right," Jord said. "Oram will have some of the women in to look at her."

Isa frowned, staring after them.

EIGHT

S he visited Seri that evening. She had doubted whether Oram would let her into their roundhouse, so she took Jord along and let him do the talking. Grudgingly, Oram let them both through the door.

Inside, the house was dark. Isa nearly choked: the air was stuffed with wood smoke and animal dung. A fire burned near the bed, where Seri lay moaning. Her sister, Sham, crouched beside her, and the old woman, Minsul, sat in a corner, chanting something under her breath. Cautiously, Isa stepped to the bed. "Seri?" She took the girl's hand, then nearly dropped it, startled at how cold it was. "Seri, how are you feeling? It's Isa. I've come to look in on you."

"She can't hear you," said Minsul. "It's the swamp sickness, from the bad water."

"Well, help her, then, if you know what it is!" Isa said. "Jord, hand me that blanket. She's ice-cold."

"Won't make a difference," Minsul said. "She won't feel it."

"Do *something*," Isa snapped.

"Nothing I can do," said Minsul. "Everyone dies, who gets the swamp sickness."

Isa stared at her. No! That couldn't be. Seri was young and strong. But then, so was Isa's brother, Tuni. *Such cruelty of the world,* she thought, *that such people should suffer.*

"Sham?" Jord said suddenly. "Sham!"

The little girl was clutching her stomach, moaning in pain, just as her sister moaned in the bed beside her. "Sham, why don't you lie down?" Isa said, hearing the panic in her own voice. "There's, that's a good girl." She looked at Minsul. "Help her."

The woman shook her head. "I told you. I can't."

Isa ground her teeth. "But surely there's something you can do to make them more comfortable! They're in such pain."

The door banged open and Tach stepped inside. "My, what a crowd," he said when he saw Isa, Jord, Minsul, and Oram. His eyes went to the bed. "What, is Sham sick, too?" He fingered the little felt bag that he had in one hand. "No matter. I have enough."

"Enough what?" Jord asked suspiciously.

"The cure for swamp sickness!" Tach said brightly; too brightly, Isa thought.

Minsul huffed, exasperated. "There *is* no cure. These girls won't last much longer."

"Of course there's a cure," Tach said, not looking at her. "Haven't you heard of it? Now, let's get them to swallow some of this." He shook the little bag.

In an instant, Oram's hand was at Tach's throat. "You'll do no such thing," he growled. "That's my wife."

"If they're going to die anyway," Isa said, glaring at Oram, "you may as well let him try."

Oram scowled, then lowered his arm. Tach slid past

him and bent over the girls. Opening the bag, he pried open Seri's mouth, then poured the bag's contents – some sort of powder – over her tongue, rubbing her throat to force her to swallow. Then he did the same with Sham.

"There's no cure for swamp sickness," Minsul muttered.

"You're a fool," Jord said to Tach. "You've no idea what that 'cure' is going to do to them. For all we know, it'll make them suffer even more."

"Maybe it will help," Isa said desperately.

"It won't." Jord's eyes smoldered. "You know why not? He isn't bragging." Jord pointed at Tach. "He always brags. If he knew this worked, he'd be praising himself to the sun, making sure he's the hero of the story."

"Jord, don't be..." Isa began.

"Oram?" They all jumped; the voice came from Seri's bed. "Oram?"

Oram leaped to her side. "Yes, Seri. I'm here."

"Could I have some water?" Seri rubbed her eyes. Her cheeks were pale, but she no longer grimaced in pain.

Within minutes, Sham was feeling better, too. "I've never seen the like," Minsul said wonderingly. "They had the swamp sickness. They were as good as dead."

Jord turned to Tach. "How did you know about the cure?" Tach bent over Seri, acting like he didn't hear. "Tach!"

"Hmm?" Tach cocked his head, but didn't turn around.

Jord leaned in close to him. "How did you know about the cure?"

"Oh, umm..." Tach still wouldn't meet his eyes. "We use this in the swamps."

"I don't think so," Jord said. "Minsul didn't know it. Nor any of the other women. A little strange that suddenly you have this magic cure no one's ever heard of."

"He's helping them," snapped Oram. "That's good enough for me."

The next day, Isa was walking in the ditch just below

the hilltop, thinking of how she might strengthen the ramparts in case of a Remi attack. Her stomach growled with hunger, so she reached into her tunic for a brittle stick of beef. She munched it absently, wincing as the wind bit into her exposed hand. No matter where she walked in these trenches, the wind cut through like a knife. *Maybe the cold will guard Cantium,* she thought. *After all, the Remi would be fools to come through this.*

Raising her head, she was surprised to see a figure in the distance, dwarfed by the sides of the ditch. Usually she met no one here, or only saw people far above on the rim. Now Isa waved at the man, but he didn't see her. He stumbled forward, bent over the uneven ground, his face covered against the wind.

It was Tach. "Where have you been?" Isa asked.

He looked up, startled to see her there. "Oh! Uh... nowhere. Out for a walk."

Isa wrapped her tunic tighter. "In this wind?"

"Oh... It's not so bad." He was about to fall over from it, and squinted his eyes as he talked to her because the wind stung them.

Isa shrugged; she would never understand swamp people. She turned to walk with him back to the hilltop. "Aren't these ramparts amazing?" she said.

Tach wrinkled his nose. "I don't think so. Big, yes, but I'd rather live in my swamps."

"Right," Isa said, laughing. "And when I met you there, you were praising Cantium."

"But think of the blood they must've spilled here," Tach said. "These trenches were dug for war. Awful! In the swamps, we never have war. I won't allow it." He lifted his head proudly. "I get my status through other means."

Blood; yes. Isa had forgotten that. She had been so captivated with being king of Cantium that it seemed unreal that the fighting would involve blood. But she couldn't worry about that right now. "Sometimes I think that we won't be ready in time," she said to Tach. "The men have been good about it all, and willing to train. But it's different down there." She gestured to the wind-swept plain far below. "We'll have only open ground between us and the Remi."

Tach followed her gaze, then shrugged. "I'm sure it'll come out right in the end."

When Isa returned the training area, Jord was waiting. He scowled at her. "Talking to Tach again?"

"Yes," Isa said. "I like him."

"I don't," Jord said firmly. "He's shifty. What's with the blinking?"

Isa rolled her eyes.

"He's always off by himself when everyone else is training," said Jord. "I don't trust him."

"That's *enough*," Isa said through her teeth. "I don't want to hear any more about it."

But the next day, Jord missed morning training, only appearing at the noon meal. "Where have you been?" Isa snapped. "You're supposed to be here helping me."

Jord smirked. "I was working in your interest, as always."

"I'm sure," said Isa. "What were you doing?"

"If you must know," Jord said, "I was checking on Tach, your so-called friend."

Isa spun on him. "Leave Tach alone!"

Jord grinned triumphantly. "I've found out what he's up to, all those times he's not at training."

"I don't want to hear it," said Isa.

"He's betraying you," said Jord.

"Enough, Jord!" Isa snapped. "Tach is loyal. Don't you slander him just because you're jealous."

But Jord persisted. The next morning, he made sure that Isa noticed when Tach laid down his weapons and strode away in the middle of battle exercises. "Off he goes," said Jord. "You need a break anyway. Always training so hard. Why don't you follow him?"

"Why don't *you* follow him?" Isa said.

Jord shook his head. "You have to see for yourself. Please, Isa. Then I'll stop bothering you about it."

Stupid man, Isa thought as she stomped off. If only she could get rid of Jord; but she needed him to lead the war training.

It was nice, though, to have some rest. Isa was used to working hard, but in June, at least, she could sing and dance at night after the long days of haying. Here there was no break in the battle preparations. Isa breathed deeply, stretching out her arms as she walked, letting the wind fill her with contentment.

After she had tramped down through the banks and ditches, she looked back. The great hill seemed small, as it had when she first came to Cantium. Isa smiled. Things felt different here on the plain; more home-like. In June, there were no dizzying heights; the world was fields, a rolling flatness just like this. Still smiling, Isa followed the plain northeast, as Jord had told her to do, until she came to a small hollow sheltered from the wind.

To her horror, she saw Tach standing with a Remi man. No! That Remi was so close; he might kill Tach. Didn't he see? Isa opened her mouth to cry out to him – but wait. Tach was talking to the man; more than that, he was laughing. "Tach!" Isa yelled. Both men jumped, startled. Isa ran to them. "Tach! What are you doing? He's the enemy! Get away from there."

"Isa!" said Tach, eyes wide. "I wasn't expecting you. This... this is Rathum."

Isa was beside him now. She jerked his arm roughly, trying to pull him away. "Why would you talk to a Remi? Haven't I told you enough? Come away!"

"It's for the sick children!" Tach cried, flinching at her grasp. "I was telling him that they're better now. That's all, Isa, really."

Isa stared at him, uncomprehending. "What are you

talking about? He doesn't care about the children. We have to get out of here, now!"

"He told me how to cure them!" said Tach. "He told me how to cure Seri and Sham."

Isa gasped. So that was how Tach had known the cure! The Remi, with their unnatural minds, had found a way to let live those who should have died, and Tach had passed off their methods as his own.

She looked at the Remi man. He was standing quietly, watching her, his breastplate glinting in the sun. "So you're trying to corrupt our children," she said. "What – to make them like you?" The Remi's eyes widened and he took a step back.

"He hasn't given me the flower!" Tach cried. "He's never given me the flower."

Isa frowned. "What's the flower?"

"The thing from the grasslands," Tach said hurriedly. He glanced at his arm, where Isa still gripped him, and began to pry away her fingers one by one. "You know, like you told me? The thing they eat that makes them so smart. It's a flower, Isa. Just a little red flower."

For a moment, Isa forgot to breathe. That was it! The answer she had sought since she had left June. She must find this flower and destroy it.

"I don't see the harm in that, Isa," Tach said, encouraged by her silence. "It's just a flower; not something that's part of them. They're not inherently bad."

"It's wrong, just the same," Isa said coldly.

"It's just a flower," Tach repeated. "Just a little thing."

Isa turned to the Remi – Rathum, Tach had called him. Isa scowled; she didn't want to know a Remi's name. What right had they to have names? They wiped out everything that was personal and human. Her anger swelled... but she had to keep her wits about her, make him tell her where to find it. "Where does this flower come from? Near here?"

"No, not here," said Rathum. His voice was deep and

husky, like his lungs had to fight for air. "They grow across the sea, in the Remi homelands." As Isa glowered at him, he added, "We eat them constantly, because they wear off after a few weeks."

"Ah! You see?" cried Tach. "It's not permanent. If it's really bad, they'll stop eating it."

"No," Rathum said. "Once you've had the flower, you can never stop."

"Why not?" said Isa.

Rathum shuddered. "You get terrible, wracking pain all over your body. It feels like you're going to die. You cry out for the flower; you go mad without it."

Isa sniffed. "Too bad it's back in your homeland, then."

"We brought some with us, with the petals dried," said Rathum. "And we're planting it."

Isa's eyes narrowed. "Planting it where?"

Rathum hesitated, then said, "In June."

Isa froze. "How dare you?" she said through her teeth. "How *dare* you?" Tach moved to calm her, but she pushed him away. "Is it not enough that you conquered us?" she cried. "You have to spread your poison, too? And now you're here, feeding gods-know-what to our children."

"I understand your concern," said Rathum. "I have kids of my own back home. I love children." He blinked. "That is, I used to. I can't remember what love feels like, since I took the flower. But I know that I loved my sons."

Isa glared at him. "Why did you leave, then, if you loved them so much?"

"We were poor," said Rathum. "There are too many of us. We were running out of land, food. And then..." He paused, swallowing. "I had forgotten love, by that time. It wasn't hard to leave them."

Isa felt sick. "That's why I'm fighting you," she said. "This flower – it makes you inhuman! What does it matter if you're smarter than us, if you can't feel love? You and your people are ruining June."

Rathum looked puzzled. "But we aren't ruining it. We're giving you towns and roads. That's why we're expanding Remi lands – not just for ourselves, but for everyone! We're civilizing you."

"If that's what you think, I don't feel sorry for you," Isa said bitterly. "Just as well that we're going to kill you all."

"Please," said Rathum. "I was just..."

"Never be seen this way again," Isa said. Then she grabbed Tach's arm and pulled him away.

NINE

They walked back across the plain, silent except for the squelching of their feet: it had begun to rain again and the ground was turning to mud. *So far from June,* Isa thought, blinking back tears. There the tall, gold grass waved in the breeze, and Isa would stride through it, exultant, feeling the sun warm on her back and letting her fingers brush the top of the grass to spread its seeds. All around her, near and far, she'd hear the scythes swinging, Zing! Zing! through the grass, and people talking, people singing, and mothers calling to children playing in the fields. But here – it was so achingly empty. Tach was with her, but she walked back to Cantium alone.

The thunder began to crash just as they reached the hill; a vicious storm, just like the night they first came to Cantium. Now Seri came running, her hair plastered to her neck from the rain. "There you are!" she said, panting. "I was worried."

"You shouldn't be up out of bed," Tach said.

"Oh, I'm fine, but look at you!" said Seri. "Absolutely drenched. Quick, come inside. We'll sit for a bit before Oram comes home." She took their arms, ready to lead them away. "You must be awfully glad to get back up here to comfort."

"Me, maybe," Isa snapped. "But not him." She gestured savagely at Tach. "He'd rather betray you. I wonder that he won't destroy this whole hill behind your backs."

Seri stared at her, open-mouthed. Isa knew her words sounded sharp, but she didn't stop to explain. Leaving Seri and Tach, she threaded through the rows of roundhouses in the gathering darkness. No one talked to her, for which she was grateful; the Cantians were too busy patching their shabby houses and bringing their grain bowls out of the rain.

Soon she came to the training area, where men were gathering the swords and spears. The ground, already torn from the feet of hapless soldiers, was a slop of mud. And there was Jord, lording it over them like the god of thunder. He smiled when he saw Isa. "Well! I suppose you saw what our friend Tach was up to. I told you he was no good. I was right, wasn't I?"

"Yes," Isa said dully.

"And to think we trusted him," Jord said, grinning. "Well, you did, anyway. I always thought there was something fishy about him. That blinking! It's like he's a creature crawled out of the swamp, waiting to belay travelers." Jord laughed harshly. "Now, as for these spears. We don't want the new lashes getting crudded up in the mud."

Pathetic, Isa thought as she looked at the water dripping from Jord's hair, at his poor useless arm, bound with sodden rags to his body. Didn't he understand? She was alone. Yes, she had friends here; but Tach had been the only one from outside, the only one not sucked into the vile stupidity of Cantium. Jord acted friendly, but he was a plotter, and he'd held up that dreadful king's skull on her first day. Even Seri was one of them. A sweet, beaming little girl; in June, she'd have run free in the fields, learning to fill her skirt with fresh-cut grasses while the sun warmed her hair. But here she coupled with a man four times her age who squeezed what little joy there was out of the day. Horrible people! Let them sit in the mud, staring into nothingness; see if Isa cared. She was done trying to change them.

"Isa," said Jord. "If we pile the spears, most of them will be kept out of the mud."

"Fine," Isa said tonelessly.

"It would be better to cover them," Jord said, "but no one's going to let a stack of spears take up his house, when it's his skin that'd be left out in the rain."

"Fine," said Isa.

Jord looked at her. "Isa? Tell me what you want. I won't pile the spears if you don't want me to."

"How would you know what I want, Jord?" she said tiredly. "Just leave me alone."

He opened his mouth, but she walked away toward her roundhouse, leaving him standing in the rain. Normally she'd stay awake for many hours, planning battle strategies with Jord, Fells, and Rye, but she didn't care; let them all rot. A thought hit her and she smiled wryly. *I've become like them: a Cantian who doesn't care.*

Someone approached her through the sheets of rain. She stepped aside to let him pass, but he stopped in front of her; drat.

"Isa, come see," Rye said excitedly. "We've a visitor."

"I don't care," said Isa. "I'm tired." It was probably some rat from the swamps; another Tach, come to make her like and trust him, only to betray her behind her back.

"No, no, you've got to see." Rye pulled her along, and Isa let him. What did it matter? She was exhausted from these weeks in dreary, useless Cantium.

On other nights, the way he took her would have been lit with fires. In the dark, the shacks would look almost grand, and she could imagine that this was Cantium of old, the great civilization, and these were the battle-hardened warriors ready to protect June and spread their songs throughout the plains. Not tonight, though. Tonight the rain dripped pitifully down from the roofs and all was dreary.

"We haven't had any visitors," Rye was saying. "Not since you and the swamp man. And this one's come from far away. You should see his tunic! Blue and gold, so very fine. I'd like it for myself, if it weren't so flimsy. He must be freezing. It's like he's never been up so high in the wind."

Isa only half-listened. *I wonder how bad the wind will get tonight,* she thought as they neared the west gate, where she and Tach had entered that first night. As on that night, people stooped over wood scraps, aiming to patch their roofs; others stood idly, talking amongst themselves even as the rain was falling. And there, in the midst of them, was Isa's brother, Batt.

Isa could not have been more shocked. The last time she saw Batt was in their parents' roundhouse, after she, Batt, Aunt, and Uncle had carried Tuni between them across the fields. Batt had been angry then, and had chastised Isa for going on a fool's errand. Rather, he'd said, that she'd stayed home and married someone, like Nuler, the potter, as a proper girl should.

Now he looked like he hadn't slept in days. Rain poured down his face and the scar on his cheek, which he'd gotten the night of the council when the Remi first came, stood in stark relief against his pale skin. A group of Cantians stood glaring at him and he glared back, not speaking. Isa pushed through the crowd, her stomach tight. Batt, here! After his disbelief in Cantium, his scoffing at her plans, his dislike of travel. His presence meant one thing: terrible news. *Someone's died,* Isa thought frantically. *Not Tuni. No, no, no!*

Now Batt saw her. "Glad that you took your time," he said sarcastically. "I've been here an hour with these buffoons. It's like they never saw a foreigner."

Isa clutched at his arm. "What's the matter? Is it Tuni?"

"No," Batt said roughly, brushing her off. "It's Father."

Father? Isa didn't understand. Father was fine, apart from his limp; there wasn't anything wrong with Father.

"The Remi took his forge," Batt said. "You know how he was about his forge. Couldn't stand for anyone to touch it. 'I'm a smith-priest,' he told them. 'You'll pay for this sacrilege. My daughter's bringing an army.' They chopped off his head with one of their steel axes."

Isa gaped. "But... no! Father can't be dead."

"This is your fault, Isa," said Batt. "You had to come here. If you'd just stayed home and not filled his head with *Cantium*" – he spat out the word – "this wouldn't have happened." Isa stared at him. Batt looked around. "I'm starving. Don't suppose there's a decent meal in this dump."

Some of the Cantians took him off to eat; Isa didn't follow. She felt numb, like the world had fallen from beneath her feet and she was still there, suspended.

Jord found her in her hut, sorting through her weapons. "Rye told me about your father," he said gently. "I'm sorry."

"Yes," she said shortly, turning from him. "Now help me pack for the battle." She picked up her sword and slid it into her belt.

"There will be time for that later," said Jord. He hugged her. "First you need to rest."

Isa pushed him away. "I can't wait. Not with this happening at home."

"I know, I know," Jord soothed.

"Tomorrow, we're going to fight these few, pitiful Remi," Isa said savagely. "And after we win, we're marching to June."

"Fine, fine," said Jord, plunking himself down on the bed. "Only wait until you're calmer. You're grieving. No need to rush a decision."

"I've decided," Isa snapped. "No more waiting! My

father's already dead. Who else has to die before you Cantians move?"

She strode out into the storm. People wandered here and there, still towing scrap wood and grain bowls. Isa called them to her. "Arm yourselves!" she cried. "We fight tomorrow! Now is the time for Cantium to rise. Reclaim your ancient glory! Tomorrow, the Remi, and afterward, June!"

Wet faces stared at her; people started whispering. "But the spears," someone said. "We haven't fixed all the spears."

"No need to hurry," said another. "With this rain, we'll have water enough for days."

"Forget all that!" Isa said. "There isn't time. We have to defeat the Remi *now*, so that we can ready ourselves to fight them in June."

"We never said we'd go to June," someone muttered.

The rain was falling faster. Isa ordered Jord, who had come behind her, to find Fells and Rye. She needed their help to spread the news. Luckily, word traveled fast in Cantium. Within minutes, everyone was talking about the battle. Satisfied that things were progressing, Isa went in search of Batt.

Through the darkness, she heard angry voices. "I won't do it," someone was saying. "I refuse."

Isa approached. "Hello?" she said. "What's the matter?"

The circle of men looked at her sullenly. "Nothing," one said.

"If there's a problem with the preparations, let me know at once," Isa said.

"We will," the man said.

But as Isa walked on, she found more groups of men talking. All fell silent as soon as they saw her, and she never quite caught their words.

Then Jord rushed up. "We've got trouble," he said urgently. "Oram's declared himself king."

"What?" Isa exclaimed. "How could he do that?"

Jord let out his breath. "He says it's his right, since you

haven't given the people what they wanted."

"But I don't understand," Isa said. "I *am* giving them what they wanted. They wanted to skip the training and fight right away. "

"Oram's giving them that, too," said Jord. "They're fighting tomorrow. Rye's organizing them now."

Isa shook her head, confused. "Then what's the point of splitting off from us? We fight tomorrow, too. I'm not keeping them from it."

Jord looked at her. "They don't want to go to June."

"Well, bother that!" Isa cried. "They can argue with me after the battle. If they don't want to go, I can't force them."

Jord pursed his lips. "It's more than that. Oram wants to take over permanently, drive you out. With him in power, you won't be safe here."

"Oh." Isa felt cold.

"Just stay here," said Jord. "I'll see what I can do. Maybe I can bring them back to our side." He gave her an encouraging smile, then vanished into the rain.

Isa couldn't stay put. What of her brother? With the Cantians against her, he could be in danger. She ran through the darkness, yelling his name.

Finally he answered from within a tumbledown hut. "Isa! What do you want?"

Isa stumbled to the door. "Batt, we're fighting tomorrow. But there's a man, Oram, who wants to lead the Cantians. He doesn't like me, and with him in charge, he might..."

"Ah, Isa, what are you going on about?" Batt appeared, looking ragged. "Such a fine night. Don't spoil it."

Isa sniffed him. "Have you been drinking?"

He grinned crookedly. "I'll say this for your Cantium: the mead ain't half bad."

Isa pulled at her hair. "Batt, we're fighting tomorrow! You have to keep your wits about you."

A woman came to the door from inside the hut: Thistle,

giggling madly. Isa stared as Batt looped his arm around her waist. "This is a fine little lady," he said, still grinning. "Come here, girl," he told Thistle. "Meet my sister."

"She knows me," said Isa, exasperated. "But you shouldn't know her. You have a wife."

Batt leaned close to her, his face suddenly dark. "Look here," he growled. "My land's overrun by savages. I've tramped through gods-know-where to get to this dump. I'm going to have my fun."

As Isa walked back to her hut, she felt overcome with emptiness. For so many nights, she had pined for her home, her tears flowing silently because she couldn't bear for strangers to hear her sobs. Now, finally, her brother was here, but he wanted nothing to do with her.

Jord was waiting at the hut. "Oram and Rye have taken half of the men," he said wearily. "But the rest are with us."

"What use is that?" Isa snarled. "You should have gotten them all back."

Jord looked at her, then said, "I'd better check the weapons. We don't want Oram making off with them all." He strode away.

Minsul emerged from the hut. "You shouldn't be so rough with him," she chided. "It's thanks to him that any are with you at all. Everyone was going to go to Oram, but Jord got them back."

"Hmph," said Isa.

TEN

Such it was that two columns of soldiers, not one, marched down from Cantium in the morning. They jeered at each other, yelling insults, for the bad blood of last night still simmered. Shouts of "King Isa!" "King Oram!" rang in the air.

Isa didn't mind the rancor as long as they all marched in the same direction. She felt like singing. Finally it was going to happen! Never mind that the Cantians said they wouldn't go to June. Once they got a taste of their old glory, they wouldn't rest. They would march to June happily.

"You shouldn't be leading a battle," said Batt beside her. His eyes were red and his hair disheveled; Thistle, still with him, hung on his arm. "Why are you even participating?" he said. "Women don't fight. Most certainly not my sister."

"Isa can do as she likes," Jord said from Isa's other side.

Batt glanced at him, then spat on the ground.

"If Tuni were here, he'd be proud of me," Isa said.

She had no patience for talk this morning. Rather, she strode exultantly, absorbing the glory of the sunrise. Below them, a blanket of fog shrouded the plain. *Lucky,* she thought. *The Remi won't see us coming.* The ground, wet from last night's rain, smelled fresh and new.

"It's Tuni's fault that you're here in the first place," Batt said. "He should do something himself for a change. If he wanted to fight the Remi, he should have come here, not you."

Isa bit her lip, but said nothing.

Thistle tossed her head. "I hope you kill many men, Batt. You're so very big and strong." She smiled, peering sideways at Jord as if to tell him that he'd missed his chance.

"Did you have to bring your whore?" Isa said to her brother.

Batt glared at her. "I wasn't going to leave her up there," he said, gesturing back at the hill. "Nasty place if I ever saw one. She'd be helpless up there if the Remi break our lines."

"Good plan," Jord said cheerfully. "Now she'll be dead if the Remi break our lines, because she'll be in them."

Thistle gave a little yelp; Batt scowled. "Who is this idiot, anyway?" he asked Isa.

Jord grinned. "Isa's future husband."

"Oh, come off it," Isa said. Even Jord couldn't irritate her this morning. She felt jubilant; soon June would be saved.

They crossed the plain in no time at all; past the copse, through the tall grass where Jord and Isa had crawled, to a short distance from the Remi camp. Isa could see the square timber houses and the river dam.

"Form up!" cried Jord.

The men got into the formations they had practiced: spearsmen in front, swordsmen behind, grouped together closely so there would be no gaps. Further from the river, by the tree where Tach had said he had napped, Oram's men were doing the same. And now the Remi were coming out of their houses, shouting at one another, and Isa could hear the clank of their swords on their metal breastplates as they pressed together, readying themselves to meet the charge.

The Cantians did charge, but the Remi rushed out, too, so fast that Isa's breath caught. No wonder the Remi had slaughtered the disheveled little force from June, that day when her brother, Tuni, was almost killed. But the Cantians were better prepared and more numerous than the men of June, and the Remi didn't push them back. The lines held: the spearsmen in front struck at the Remi, felling them before they could get within reach with their steel swords.

Those who did get through found their matches in the Cantian swordsmen. Had the numbers been equal, the Remi would have massacred them, but with three or four Cantians for every Remi, the Remi couldn't advance, though they cut mightily with their steel. The two sides were stuck together, engaged head-on like in the great battles of old. It all might have made for a stirring song.

Except for the blood. Oh, gods, Isa couldn't bear the blood. It was everywhere: spurting from the Remi men that she struck, from the Cantian soldiers in the line beside her. She had thought that swinging the sword would be like swinging the scythe; but instead of chopping grass, she was chopping men.

Someone else's blood spattered on her cheeks and in her mouth, and she cried out in horror. As the bile rose in her throat, she slowed the pace of her cuts, bringing her sword almost to a stop – but no, she couldn't; the Remi were still coming on. She must hack and hew at them, or get cut with a sword herself. She gagged, choking. Her sword arm burned; however strong she was, she wasn't strong enough for this fighting. Each time her sword hit a Remi breastplate, a shock went up her arm: a dreadful pain like her bones were breaking and her teeth were knocking around in her head.

Yet still the Remi came. They and the Cantians were locked in a standstill. It all seemed to move so slowly. Isa was aware of everything: the pungent smell of human sweat, the grunting soldiers, Fells and Jord and all the others around her. These were people she saw every day doing ordinary things. She'd thought that battle would be mythic, that the sky would look different somehow; but it looked just the same, and the ground felt the same beneath her. *Battle must be ordinary, then,* she thought dazedly. *Just another happening on another day.*

But the smell of the blood overwhelmed her, pressing against her nose and lungs. She had some of it on her tongue, tangy and sharp. She was stumbling, bent over at the waist – then Jord's hand was on her shoulder and he was pulling her back. They were all moving back, all the Cantians in her line.

"Why?" she said, confused. "Why are we going back?"

"Oram's retreating," said Jord. "I don't know why. But we can't match the Remi without Oram's men. We'll have to do whatever he does."

In no time, they were in the copse. Isa peered through the fog; she had thought the battle had gone on for hours, but the sun hadn't moved at all. She gasped, trying to force air back into her battered lungs.

"Come," Jord whispered, motioning to her. "There's scant cover here."

He was right; the trees were bare already, with none of summer's lush green to shield them from the Remi. Isa staggered after Jord through the mud and rotting leaves. He seemed at home here; his eyes were bright, darting every way, seeing through the fog and the shadows.

He will save them, Isa thought suddenly as she fell to her knees. *Jord will save the Cantians, and later he will save June.* She knew this as she huddled on the ground, miserable and powerless. All the airs that she had given herself these past few weeks, strutting around Cantium as king, meant nothing. She saw that now. She was feeble, not strong. If ever the Remi would be defeated, Jord would be the one to do it, or someone like him; not Isa.

She couldn't see the Cantian soldiers around her, but she could hear them. Feet crunched on fallen branches; muffled voices called through the trees: "Help me!" "Why'd we pull back?" "We lost so many!" "Cantium is fallen. It's over."

Jord's voice cut through the others' despair: "No! It's not over. Keep moving. We can still win!"

A few men answered him, attempting faint cheers. Jord stepped back to where Isa crouched in the mud. *Now is his moment,* she thought, gazing up at him. Jord could kill her right there and say that she died in the battle, then take her ring and proclaim himself king; he could even say that it was her dying wish for him to succeed. What was to stop him? *How foolish of me,* she thought piteously. *Putting my trust in these strangers. If our world is doomed, I should be living my last days with my family, not all alone here in this wind and cold.*

And where was her brother, Batt? She hadn't seen him since the battle started. She vaguely remembered him in the line, hacking and hewing with the rest of them. Where was he now? He was her only connection to the home that she had lost. Now she was alone among Cantians and Jord was going to kill her. He leaned down, peering at her face. Isa braced herself.

"Are you all right?" he said anxiously. "Please, Isa. Are you hurt? Have you been wounded?"

"No," she said, confused. Wasn't he going to do it?

Jord squeezed her hand. "Do you want to press on? Or fall back? I think we can beat them, but it's up to you. Say the word, and I'll obey."

He was awaiting her orders, not usurping! *Silly Jord,* she thought at the back of her mind. *You should usurp. I'm nothing; I'm weak. You're the one with all the power, who knows how to manage this, who feels at home in this damp, stinking rot, amid all the blood.* "Go on," she croaked. "Go on. Let's beat them."

"Come with me, then," he said. "The men will want to see you."

Isa stared at him, uncomprehending. "Lead them?" she moaned. " No. I can't."

"You don't have to do anything," Jord said soothingly. "Just stand up, walk with me, so they can see you. Then the victory will be yours. They'll worship you, and you'll be safe."

"Safe?" Isa's thoughts were muddled; she couldn't see straight.

"Yes," said Jord. "If they worship you, they'll gladly defend you against Oram. I don't trust them otherwise." He looped his good arm around Isa's waist. "Come now. I'll help you." In one motion, he pulled her to her feet.

Isa shook her head, trying to clear her dizziness. She saw that Jord's injured arm hung at his side, having fallen out of the fold in his tunic where he had tucked it. Blood seeped from the original wound at his shoulder. Gritting her teeth, Isa reached for Jord, gingerly tucking in his arm again so that he wouldn't do further damage. This was her life now, she thought, whether or not she liked it. These hard, rough people were strangers – and yet Jord watched over her while her brother was nowhere to be found.

Men gathered around. Eager faces thrust in front of Isa, seemingly glad to see her. "Look, there are Oram's men," someone said.

"Tach, take a message to Oram," said Jord. Isa jumped; she hadn't known that Tach was there, fighting the Remi with the rest of them. "Tell him to form a wing and come on them from the side while we take them from the front."

Tach scurried off, low against the ground. Isa balled her hand against her mouth. Tach had befriended that Remi, Rathum, and wanted Isa to see his humanity. The Remi were unnatural; Isa knew that, and she had killed them. And yet their flesh felt human enough under her sword.

Tach returned. "He won't do it."

"Damn him," Jord muttered. "Our forces are each too small to beat the Remi alone."

"Send another messenger," said Fells. "He won't listen to Tach because he's not Cantian."

So Fells went over; but still Oram refused.

"We're going to lose," cried Isa. "Oh, gods, we're going to lose."

"Not yet," Jord said firmly. "Oram seems to be moving east. If we move north, we can help him pen them in against the river."

Isa saw little of that second battle. She tried to run with the others, but her lungs were burning white-hot fire. The muscles in her sword arm screamed; it was all she could do to stand in place holding it. *Come to me,* she thought wildly. *Come to me, Remi, so I don't have to run all that way to kill you.*

Then came the shouts: "We've won! We've won!" "Cantium is saved!" Isa struggled toward the sound. Could it be true? She felt strangely empty.

A figure lurched toward her through the fog. In the eerie light, it looked like some spirit from the underworld. Isa gripped her sword.

"Oh!" the person gasped.

Isa peered closer. It was Rathum, the Remi. He was limping from a wound to his side. He waved his hands. "Please, Isa. Don't kill me."

Rage welled up inside her. "Why shouldn't I?" she spat out. "Your people hurt my brother, made my father die in disgrace." She stepped closer to him, menacing. "Why shouldn't I do to you what you did to them?"

Rathum cringed away. "Please."

Isa raised her sword.

A hand grasped her shoulder. "No need for that," Jord

said gently. "We've won."

Isa gritted her teeth. "I'm going to do it. You can't stop me."

All she could see was red. She imagined hacking in a fury, panting, screaming. *Yes, I will kill them! I will destroy them all.*

Tach appeared behind Jord. "Have some mercy, Isa!" he said urgently. "They're people, too."

"No, they're not!" said Isa, faltering. "They're nothing like us. They can't even remember how to love."

"Then don't be like them," Tach said.

Isa ground her teeth. "Bind him up," she told Jord, motioning at Rathum. "He's our prisoner."

Jord grinned. "As you say."

"Thank you," gasped Rathum.

Isa turned away. "Just be quiet."

"That was good of you," said Tach, following her. "He has children."

"Maybe they all have children," Isa said tiredly. "But we do, too."

ELEVEN

*M*en swarmed around now, clapping Isa on the back and cheering. Blood had spattered on their teeth, and their faces wore the ugliness of battle: rage, weariness, and blood-lust. More men milled around Jord and the prisoner, Rathum.

"Did you see her?" someone said excitedly. "Cutting down all those men in the battle line."

"Aye, and she led the charge through the copse," said another. "She slew dozens and dozens of them."

"A true foe for the enemy!" Fells cried, raising his sword. "All the times of old, they had their mythic kings. But we have our *woman* king, our Isa!"

"Ai!" cried the men.

"I didn't do half the things they say I did," Isa murmured to Jord when he was near.

"Doesn't matter," he said firmly. "Now you'll be safe

with them."

Isa saw Tach standing off to the side, silently watching her. He looked away when she met his gaze. Isa went to him, avoiding those men who tried to lift her into the air in celebration. What to say to Tach? She hardly knew.

"Thank you for fighting," she said softly. Tach sniffed, but said nothing. Isa tried again. "I know you didn't want to. You were brave to fight them, just the same."

"It's not that," Tach said testily. "I'm not afraid to fight. I used to fight all the time, to protect the swamp. I've fought off raiders all alone."

"Of course," Isa said quickly. "I meant no offense. Just... thank you. And I'm sorry." She took a breath. "It was awful. The blood; the Remi. I know they're evil... but still. I could hardly bear to do it."

He blinked at her, then smiled wanly. "I know what terrible things they've done to your people," he said. "But that first time I saw Rathum..." He paused, staring off across the plain. "I pitied him. He was so alone. He needed someone to understand."

Isa patted his arm. Dear Tach! "You always do that, don't you?" she said. He raised his eyebrows. "Pity people," she explained. "You give sympathy to the downtrodden, even when others don't see the need."

Tach grinned. "Why do you think I helped you get to Cantium?"

Isa started. Then she laughed shakily. "Yes, I suppose I was rather a hopeless cause, staggering up from June with my head stuffed full of dreams."

"I'm glad we're friends again," Tach said. "But look." He nodded behind her. "Someone to see you."

Isa turned. "Batt! You're safe! Thank the gods." She ran to her brother, folding herself into his arms.

"Well, it wasn't any thanks to your Cantians," Batt said. "All that carnage! So uncivilized. I'm shocked that you've gotten yourself into this." But he let her hug him, not pushing her away.

"Batt, dearest darling!" Thistle flounced up, pouting. "You promised you wouldn't leave me."

"It's fine. I'm here," Batt said soothingly.

"Oh, but I was frightened!" Thistle cried, clutching him.

"There, now," Batt said, taking her in his arms.

"And all those scary men," Thistle said. "I thought I was going to die." She glanced at Isa, then, almost imperceptibly, moved between Isa and Batt. Slowly, she began to lead Batt away.

Isa watched them sadly. She couldn't even enjoy her brother; Thistle owned him now. But she felt more relaxed with Tach and Jord, anyway, than with Batt.

The soldiers were gathering their gory weapons and heading back, streaming toward the Cantium hill.

"What about June?" Isa said. "Remember we're going to June."

Men glanced at her, but kept watching. "June ain't our land," someone said. "This is."

"But the battle!" Isa said desperately. "You all loved the battle."

"That's enough for me," said Fells. "Now, time for a feast!"

They were all moving away, ignoring Isa when she called to them. *No hope for June now,* she thought. What was it for, then, all this blood? Blood that she, Isa, had brought.

"Gods!" a man exclaimed. "You startled me there." He had stumbled over someone in the high grass: Rye, on his hands and knees.

Jord scowled down at him. "What are you doing?"

"Uh... Crawling," said Rye.

Jord hauled him to his feet, making Rye yelp. "Why were you crawling?" Jord demanded.

Rye glared at him. "Well, I didn't want you to see me, did I? Traitors, the lot of you. I fell behind my column and

I'm just trying to get back to Oram."

"Traitors?" Jord said, his eyes dark. "Seems to me that you're the one who's a traitor."

Rye shoved by him roughly. "Just let me pass. I want to walk with my own kind."

"Don't get in a prickle," Fells said. "We're all going in the same direction."

Jord still glowered at Rye. "You went against Isa. I told you not to think of it. Not ever."

"It's all right, Jord," Isa said. "What does it matter now?" Yet somehow she felt warm; she was glad that Jord had never been against her.

"It's like Jord to be an ogre about it," Rye grumbled. "Do you know, when we were ten years old..."

"What's this?" Jord said, interrupting.

Something was happening at the front of the line, which had snaked up the hill almost to the east gate. Men were shouting and holding their heads. Isa saw a tongue of flame hurtle through the air and strike a man to the ground.

"Fire spears!" Jord yelled. "Fall back!"

The men bunched together in confusion. Rocks were flying, too, Isa saw, propelled from the stores within the ramparts that they had put there to ward off the Remi.

"Oram's taken the hill!" Fells shouted. "They've cut us off."

"But why?" Isa said, incredulous. "You're all Cantians. How could they shut out their own people?"

Jord scowled up at the east gate, where heads began to appear, taunting them. "For power," he said. "There can't be two kings of Cantium. Now Oram thinks he's the only one."

Cries of fear rippled among the men. Some made forays toward the gate, but Oram's men forced them back, knocking some unconscious with the rocks.

"My wife is up there!" one man cried.

"Aye, and mine," said another. "My children, too."

Batt smirked. "Now I'm looking smart, bringing Thistle

down with me," he said. "Bet you all wish you'd done the same."

No one paid attention to him. Isa ground her teeth in frustration; the very fortifications they had worked so hard to prepare were being used against them. The men were frantic, exhausted from the battle, wanting only to go home. But now Oram himself appeared at the gate.

"We'll never let you in!" he shouted, prompting cheers from his men. "That's your punishment for following *her*, your maiden king!"

"But I'm one of you!" Rye cried. "I'm on your side, I fought with you. Let me in!" He rushed forward, but a flaming spear flew to meet him, narrowly missing. Fells and Jord dragged him back out of range. "No!" Rye cried. "They have to let me in! I can't be stuck out here with you."

"We're the least of your problems," said Fells. "We'll starve out here. They've got all the grain, and most of the animals, too."

"We could all go up at once," someone said. "Storm the hill."

"No," said Jord, shaking his head. "That would be suicide. Those defenses are strong; they were meant for the Remi. Oram would slaughter us."

"Go south, then," Tach said softly. Isa looked at him. "To a different place, with a longer growing season."

"We'll have to face another battle anyway," Jord said to the men. "Either we march up there and fight our cousins and brothers" – he gestured at the hill – "or we go with Isa to June. I don't know about you, but I'd rather kill a bunch of Remi than my own kin."

"Yes, yes, June," men began to say reluctantly. "Might as well."

"We'll fight for honor!" Fells said, his face pale. "The old Cantian honor. There's nothing else left, without our home."

"Yes!" cried Rye. "We must go to June! Wipe out the

Remi there, then bring back the men of June to drive these brutes off our hill." He spat in Oram's direction, though the man had vanished behind the gate.

That was it, then; the end of Isa's stay in Cantium. She felt no joy at this moment, as she had once imagined she would. As she tramped beside the listless men, she thought of giving a speech to goad their spirits, but decided against it. Whatever she did had little effect; events moved of their own accord.

A thought struck her. "Seri!" she cried. "Seri's up on the hill."

"We'll have to leave her," Jord said, not unkindly. "Oram will look after her."

Isa glanced back at the hill, where it stretched out, slumbering, its true vastness hidden once again. It didn't seem as empty as it had when she first came; not after all that effort and striving. Perhaps she would return one day, after all. But first, to June.

She pictured the sun rising over the fields, pale-gold in the morning light. With the harvest in, people would be readying for winter, that time of leisure and laughter and stories. The Remi ruled them now, but here was half of Cantium coming to save them. Isa raised her face to the sky, and smiled.

EPILOGUE

A good victory for Isa, but still I have much to tell. I, Imon, must write of the fall, the horror, the darkness.

Here on the old hill, day is dawning. I must go down soon, or they will see me: my people, the Cantians – or the Remi. Who it is does not matter; we are the same now. Ah, to have lived in the time before we lost everything!

But day is dawning. From on high, I see the plains spread out below me, hinting of the glory of man. I will write of these vistas, and they will remember.

Isa will live through me.

AUTHOR'S END NOTE

Cantium, though fictionalized here, was a real place: the present-day county of Kent in southeast England. I took the name from Julius Caesar's *Gallic Wars*, which mentions four kings of Cantium who ruled at the time of Caesar's expedition to Britain in 54 BC.

These were Iron Age kings, each ruling from a hill-fort – a fortified center of population, production, and culture. Of all the British tribes, Caesar says, the Cantians were the most civilized.

The Remi in *The Kings of Cantium* are rather like the Romans: foreign invaders with superior weapons and equipment and more systematized ways of doing things. Rome had conquered Iron Age Britain by the end of the first century AD.

The real-life Remi were a people of northeastern Gaul (modern France). Allying themselves with Julius Caesar, they fought other Gallic tribes when most of the tribes rebelled against Rome. The Remi were a warlike people, famous for their horses. Later, after they were absorbed into the Roman Empire, Remi troops fought in many of Rome's campaigns, including, probably, the conquest of Britain.

The events of this book, though, are entirely of my own invention. I could have written a strictly historical novel, but wanted to allow my imagination free room to play.

WHY THE IRON AGE?

My fascination with the Iron Age (800BC – 50AD in Europe) began while I was a student at Oxford, when I would take the train out to sites in the British countryside. On one of my wanderings, I found Old Sarum, a little hill outside the cathedral city of Salisbury. Sheep graze on it now, but people have used it continuously for 5,000 years, including in the Iron Age, when it was a hill-fort.

As I stood on the hill, watching clouds billow over the plains, I felt the incredible oldness of the place. The patchwork fields below had the same boundaries as they did in the Iron Age, and before, despite all the changes that came after. I imagined that people have remained the same, too – still striving to live under the same sky.

That day in 2006, stories began to stir within me. I would write of a great civilization, once lost, rising again – because, walking within that epic landscape, it felt like the past could come back to life. Each step I took on the hilltop was a testament to the endurance of mankind. From hunter-gathering to farming to the modern age, it all happened on that same ground, one layer of time atop another.

I visited other hill-forts that first year in England; always, they were places of meditation and exuberant thoughts. At the White Horse Hill, in Oxfordshire, I watched a thunderstorm roll in across the plain. The town was far below along an open road, but a hundred yards above was an Iron Age ditch, part of the ramparts that defended the hill from invaders. So I crouched in the ditch and ate my lunch while lightning flashed, imagining an Iron Age person sheltering in that same spot during a storm.

On a hill-fort, you feel separate from yourself – or rather, like your greatest self: you can spread your arms, stride alone for what seems like miles, imagining your own epic deeds. Is it any wonder, then, that hill-forts help me spin epic stories? When I left England, though, after my year abroad, I was still waiting, not yet confident enough as a writer.

Fast-forward to early 2009, after I'd returned to the U.K. as a graduate student at St Andrews in Scotland. January of that year was depressing: I was homesick, missing the glory of my old journeys from Oxford, wanting something to inspire me again. So where to go? To a hill-fort, of course!

I traveled to Maiden Castle in southern England, the largest hill-fort in Britain, which became the model for Cantium in the book. In fact, I wrote the first sketch of the story on top of Maiden, leaning over my notebook for hours in the wind. It was wonderful to finally write the story that had begun in my mind at Old Sarum.

It's taken me four years since then to develop a writer's work ethic, to learn how to finish the things that I started, but late is always better than never.

ABOUT THE AUTHOR

Erica Olson was born in St. Paul, Minnesota, and, after various moves around Montana and Idaho, grew up in Plains, Montana, population 1,050. As a child, she loved to write stories about talking animals (usually horses or wolves.)

In 2003, Erica left for Philadelphia to attend the University of Pennsylvania. She spent a year abroad at Oxford University in England, where she imagined that she walked in the steps of great people and that she would achieve greatness, too. While at Oxford, she filled countless notebook pages with philosophical musings and the seeds of stories.

Erica graduated from Penn in 2007 with a major in European history and a minor in philosophy. In 2008, she left for graduate school in St Andrews, Scotland, now studying Classics (ancient Greek and Roman history, literature, and language). She wanted to study the past in order to create and develop her own ideas. Next, she studied for and received a second Master's degree, in English literature, from Washington State University, having wanted to return to her rural Western roots. Her thesis was about how contemporary literature might explore positive ideals of human striving.

Erica lives in Plains, Montana, where she writes, runs, and plays with her dogs.

COMING SOON:

THE NEXT ALLIANCE
*The Kings of Cantium,
Book Two*

FOR DETAILS, VISIT
WWW.ERICA-OLSON.COM

ALSO BY ERICA OLSON:

A LONDON TALE

eBook, March 2012

In this dreamlike vision of London, a ruthless general-turned-eccentric composer searches for a stolen symphony, his greatest work. With a patient friend and an old enemy, he takes on a pair of taunting brothers and confronts past pain, cruelty, and his own lust for power. He roams an irrational city: amidst echoes of wars real and imaginary, the 19th century mixes with the modern present. In a world where Christmas ("Godmas" in the story) celebrates humanity within an impersonal universe, can he learn the value of friendship and forgiveness?

WWW.ERICA-OLSON.COM

Lightning Source UK Ltd.
Milton Keynes UK
UKHW021827311018
331547UK00026B/467/P